A SHORT WALK TO THE SEA

SHORT STORIES BY

EDDY KNIGHT

Truth Serum Press
32 Meredith Street
Sefton Park SA 5083
Australia

Email: truthserumpress@live.com.au
Website: http://truthserumpress.net
Truth Serum Press catalogue:
http://truthserumpress.net/catalogue/

Cover design copyright © Matt Potter
Front cover photograph copyright © AnnaER
Author photograph copyright © Justene Knight and used with permission

ISBN: 978-1-925536-01-0

Also available as an eBook
ISBN: 978-1-925536-02-7

Truth Serum Press is a member of the
Bequem Publishing collective

http://www.bequempublishing.com/

CONTENTS

THE AUTHOR

I wanted the author to come to my house. I had wanted him to come for such a long time.

I was walking along Semaphore beach one blustery winter's morning when I recognised him from the photos on the backs of his books. He marched along the strand, his boots crunching shells washed up above the tide line, rugged up in a woollen coat with a scarf wrapped around his ears and mouth, into which he mumbled words. I couldn't make out what he was saying above the sloughing of the sea and the crackling beneath his feet, but he was definitely putting voice to some internal monologue. A portion of a story he was working on perhaps, a section of some forthcoming masterwork, so I dared not rush up and interrupt him.

Of course he could have just been revisiting an argument he'd had that morning with his wife, considering improved ripostes that he should have made over their morning tea and toast. We all experience the frustration of the delayed comeback from time to time, but surely not him I thought, not with his felicity with language.

My watch told me it was 10 o'clock. I determined to return at the same time on subsequent days in hope of running into him again. Lying in wait you might say; stalking is too provocative a term when all that I was hoping for was the briefest of conversations. A structural ambush perhaps. The opportunity to express my admiration for his works. He was an accomplished author, had published numerous novels, won a plethora of the country's most prestigious literary prizes and awards. I was a mere scribbler by comparison, a crafter of much more modest fictions, an entrant into story competitions with, as yet, no greater success than a short-listing or two. We were not operating on the same level, I knew that only too well, but still...

For several weeks he did not reappear. The weather broke. Finally spring came round with warmer winds and placid seas. Walking the beach had become my daily discipline, an opportunity to investigate ideas and play with possibilities, much as the black-capped terns played with the water, snatching whatever fish they spotted gliding beneath its surface. Removal from my study, with its cluttered desk and the accusation of an often blank computer screen lent an improved perspective to my own creative efforts. But however much I enjoyed the stimulus of breathing ozone, of walking barefoot and wriggling my toes in the warmth of golden sand, I was still looking out for him, still eagerly hoping for a chance encounter.

Finally he was there again, overcoat and scarf long since discarded with the temperature reaching towards the thirties. Sunglasses, jeans and T-shirt, with a leather satchel hanging from one shoulder, looking considerably younger than his sixty-odd years. I approached him and began to raise a hand in salutation when my nerve failed me. Embarrassed at my timidity, overwhelmed by twinges of envy, I redirected my hand to sweep the hair out from my eyes. I stumbled an impersonal 'good morning', but that was all. He must have noticed my mouth opening and closing for he nodded and smiled in my direction although he could not have heard. There were wires descending from a pair of ear buds snaking into his satchel and as I passed I heard a tinny rendition of orchestral music. Debussy I thought, fittingly for our situation *La Mer*, one of my personal favourites.

What exactly was it that I was after? It had to be more than mere conversation. I wanted him to come to my house, to grace my study with his presence, as if some beneficence might be bestowed upon the room by his fleeting occupancy, some trace left behind after his departure, as incense lingers long after it has burnt. My narrow room feels like a monastic cell on occasion; a small rug upon the concrete floor, a desk, an armchair, a wall of books and, between the windows, a doorway which leads out into the secluded garden. My partner rarely intrudes, and no one else, ever. I wanted *him* to. Imagined him sitting in the armchair, crossing his legs as he surveyed the contents of the bookshelves and admired the breadth of my reading. We could discuss his preferences. Would he ask about my own work?

I realised that I had none of his books upon my shelves. He was so renowned they were easy to borrow from the library. I could hardly expect him to sit with equanimity next to such a collection of contemporary fiction, when he was not represented. He was bound to notice. The visit would not go well. He would be offended, leap to his feet, utter some scathing remark and leave.

I ordered what I considered his most successful novel over the internet. That was when I formulated my plan. The perfect excuse.

Come the summer we were both in shorts. He was wading through water up to his knees, laughing like a child as waves threatened further encroachment. I kicked off my shoes and paddled out to greet him. I told him of my latest acquisition.

"Would you come home for a cup of tea, and sign it for me?"

I was shocked by his response. My mouth, fish-like, remained half open.

"Of course," he said. "I would be delighted."

I AM HERE

They had been best of friends for, like, ages. Ever since the first year of Le Fevre High. Together they had pulled girls' pony tails, nicked fruit from people's gardens, wagged school and spent the day at the beach. Then, later on, kissed and fumbled with the self-same girls, smoked furtive cigarettes behind the demountable classroom, wagged school and spent the day at the beach. They even lived in the same street, Jack down one end of Hargrave Street, the cement works end near Victoria Road, and Tom up the other end by Military Road, the end closest to the beach. So, after a day spent fishing, or perving on young mothers in bikinis laid out tantalisingly upon the golden sands, they would walk back to Tom's place together to play some Xbox. Then Jack would carry on home for his tea.

They were both given bikes on the same Christmas so could roam somewhat further afield; down along the peninsula to admire the yachts at North Haven marina or up to the BMX track near the posh newer houses of the West Lakes development. Tom's was a proper BMX machine whereas Jack's was a second hand road bike from Cash Converters but it didn't really matter, for they would take turns on Tom's, launching themselves skyward from the artificial humps or making sharp braking turns to spray up dirt and gravel.

Tom's mother didn't like Jack much, considered him a bad influence on her precious boy. It wasn't true, of course, that was just the way that mothers were. Tom knew only too well that if there was any bad influencing going on it was in totally the other direction. He was the boss of their little two-man crew. It was he who decided what any day's particular activities would consist of, he who bought the fags and later on the aerosol cans of spray paint. After all it was he who had the pocket money, supplemented on occasion by the odd surreptitious raid on his mother's purse, carried out when he considered that she had drunk enough chardonnay to be unable to remember the contents precisely. For all the influence that he was able to exert on his friend this was the one thing that he could never get Jack to attempt with his own mother's purse. However often he would laugh and call him "chicken" he always got the same answer.

"She'll know," Jack would insist.

Indeed Wendy probably would have, never having much in there in the first place. This was not the real reason, however. Jack was only too aware of just how hard his mother had to work at her various cleaning jobs in order to feed and clothe the two of them, of how long she had had to scrimp to get him that bike he had so desperately wanted. He had accompanied her on a few occasions in the school holidays. To see his mother on her knees cleaning someone else's toilet hurt him in some deep place that he would never dream of trying to explain to Tom. To steal from his own mother was unthinkable, tantamount to stealing from himself.

He had no such qualms about benefitting from his friend's nefarious activities though, and happily joined in the laughter when Tom described his mother as "the glamorous bank". Well it was pretty funny, because she did work in a bank, and as far as Jack was concerned she was very glamorous. For a forty-year-old, anyway. Always immaculately made up and attractively dressed when she returned from work in her dark business suits over white blouses, black stockings emphasising the shapeliness of her legs. She was the most glamorous woman that he could think of, apart from in pictures and on the telly of course, although he never admitted as much to his friend, rather gratefully accepting the odd ice-cream, the occasional cigarette, the fruits of her unknowing beneficence.

Another bond between them was the absence of fathers. Tom's was still around, just in a different home. At the age of thirty-nine he had traded his wife in on a new model, as he expressed it to his cronies at golf, or in the smoking room of the Adelaide Club. 'The Bimbo' Tom called her, taking after his slighted mother, although this was not strictly fair. She was just younger, that was all, with firmer breasts, a tauter stomach and so far an absence of stretch marks. She had been a legal secretary in his father's practice and, as is the way with some working relationships it had gradually developed into something else. The fact that Tom senior often had to travel up country and inter-state on various clients' business, requiring her secretarial support, had somewhat inevitably led to support of a more intimate nature. Just because she was a minion he wouldn't have dreamt of accommodating his very attractive, young clerk elsewhere than in his own luxurious hotels, so they often dined together, imbibed afterwards in the lounge together and very shortly shared the same room, the same bed, together.

So at the age of nine Tom, with his mother, had relocated from their Tusmore home to the slightly more modest Federation style house down on the peninsula. It had once been the holiday home of a wealthy Adelaide businessman who, like a lot of his contemporaries, had it built around the turn of the twentieth century to spare his family the oppressive summer heat of the city. In an era before air-conditioning the coastal strip had housed many such families once the temperature rose above thirty degrees and started inexorably to head for the forties. The wives and children could relax and enjoy the beach whilst the husbands would travel the ten miles to the city and back again in the relative comfort of the newly-built train. The onshore breeze in the evenings rendered family life much more bearable for all.

Further back from the beach, towards the Port River side of the peninsula, the houses became increasingly more modest, timber framing clad with corrugated iron, the metal frontages pressed to resemble the stonework of their grander neighbours. These had housed the workers, the myriad of craftsmen, lumpers and assorted labourers once necessary for the commercial success of such a bustling port. Jack's house was one of these, its original metal exterior supplemented in the fifties by fibro extensions at the rear to accommodate a bathroom and an inside toilet.

Jack's father, only recently married, had not absconded from the marital bed. His absence was the result of an industrial accident at the soda ash plant where he had worked for only a few years. Mostly his fault, so the tribunal declared, the result of skylarking in the presence of dangerous chemicals, sulphuric acid to be precise. So the compensation payout was not very large, and took an awfully long time to arrive. Wendy with her two-year-old son had had to scrape along on a miniscule pension whilst she worked out what she could do. Luckily the house had been bought just before the rise in property values. Besides which, being in the shadow of the cement works and so close to the busy main road that semi-trailers roared down day and night, transporting containers to and from the terminal at the tip of the peninsula, the mortgage hadn't been large. With a little help from her parents, her father having a good job as a deckhand on one of the tugs, she had managed to hold on to it until the laughably small payout finally arrived and they were assured of continuing occupancy. "Was this all that a life was worth?" she had thought, in the bitterness of her nights.

Jack had no memory of his father beyond the wedding photograph in its hardwood frame which had once graced the living room mantelpiece, before one day disappearing into an album somewhere. He hadn't asked. A ginger-top was all that he knew, as he was himself, the curly luxuriance of which had earned him the nickname of 'ranga' at school. When Tom had finally arrived in his class it was a relief to have someone who had called him Jack.

The aerosol cans had been purchased from a cousin of Tom's, a man who worked in an auto repair shop and who thought that his aunt's ex-husband was a shit. The boys were both sixteen years old by now and had got themselves into hip-hop. They wore American style truck drivers' caps, with the peaks slanted in what they considered an acceptably rakish angle, and trousers that rode so low on their hips the elastic waists of their underpants showed, and the crutches hung down towards their knees so that when they walked it looked like they'd crapped in their pants.

Art was the only subject that interested Tom in school, while Jack was more into wood and metal-work. He had brought home to his mother the occasional breadboard, some pairs of bookends which could hold up her magazines, and once an elaborate poker for the fire. Neither knew what the approaching end of their school careers would bring.

Tom had had a project in mind for a number of months, an expression of devotion to the super-heroes who fought their way through his Marvel comics. A mural, a work of public art. As he explained it to Jack it would beautify the neighbourhood, while leaving a lasting tribute to their skill and their daring, permanent evidence of their inner worth. Jack was all for it. Although not particularly artistic himself, if Tom could execute a suitable outline he could take part in the colouring-in. They would have to invent tags for themselves, so they could sign the masterpiece incognito when it was finished. No one in authority would know who had done it, but they would, and be proud. It would be something they could boast about at school.

Almost half way between their two houses was Peterhead station, with a fine tin fence that faced the platform for town. This, they agreed, would be the perfect site. It had been graffitied before; clumsy, amateurish attempts of no artistic value, which no one had bothered cleaning up. They would paint over these childish squiggles, these infantile declarations of love for Sara by Brett, or Marky for Mel. It would improve the quality of life for the daily commuters as they stood gazing upon their colourful creation and wondering just who could have executed such a marvellous thing.

Whilst they gradually amassed an assortment of spray cans Tom pondered which of his heroes should figure in their mural. In the end he realised that it was really no contest. Captain America symbolised all of their aspirations; the man with the shield who defended pure and innocent individuals from the evil machinations of criminal gangs, hell-bent on destroying God's-own way of life. With that settled he started on a few preliminary sketches, copying from his comics a number of characteristic poses. Eventually, in consultation with Jack, he settled on one where their gigantic protagonist stood proudly straddling the numerous crumpled bodies of his dark, faceless and defeated foes.

Luckily for them, at Peterhead station both the up and the down Outer Harbour line trains arrive within a few minutes of each other. This gave them almost hour-long bursts of feverish activity before having to scramble back across the track and hide in the rudimentary urine-smelling shelter up on the platform. It grew dark about eight and by that time most of the workers had returned from their jobs and any evening revellers had departed for town. Should anyone disembark after that the boys would pretend they were awaiting the other train.

The platform lights designed to protect potential travellers and to cut down on vandalism gave them sufficient illumination and the work went well. There was always plenty of warning of an oncoming train from the clanging of bells and flashing red lights which heralded barriers dropping across Wills or Harris Streets. About eleven o'clock Jack did trip over one of the rails but the fall didn't knock him completely senseless and, somewhat dazed, he managed to pull himself up onto the platform before being caught in the glaring eyes of the approaching diesel behemoth. Meanwhile Tom was frantically scrambling about, searching for the scattered cans that Jack had been carrying in the sack. He missed one in the shadow cast by the raised platform's edge but luckily it had rolled out of danger and was not crushed or exploded under one of the wheels. The only damage was a small cut above Jack's left eye and the boys both laughed at their near shave with disaster. When the train pulled out, having disgorged no passengers, they leaped down onto the track once again, adrenaline pumping, and set about resuming their work.

Tom did the finer work of course, having a steadier hand and a firmer grasp of the overall construction. Jack filled in larger blocks of colour and the shadowy, indistinct creatures lying crushed beneath the Captain's feet. Finally came the shield, of which Tom was particularly proud, great glossy symbol as it was of the truth, of justice and of the American way. Standing back, finally, after the 12.15 had rumbled off, they were able to take in the enormity of their achievement, the eight foot high magnificent crime fighter, resplendently garbed in his red, white and blue, his glowing eyes burning through the slits in his mask, daring oppression to come. They stood and they gazed and they high-fived for minutes, before jumping back down on the track and appending the tags they'd worked out. Tom's was an indecipherable squiggle whilst Jack's a combination of his three initials each superimposed upon the other. All in all it had been a brilliant night's work, and they returned to their homes, chests swollen and brains near bursting with joy.

Jack rose early the following day, and set off shortly after breakfast. Wendy was surprised as he was not habitually an early riser, but she put it down to the excitement of his last week of school. In fact he went to check that their portrait of the illustrious Captain looked as fine in the early morning as it had seemed to do last night. He wasn't disappointed, and revelled in the excited comments of a few of the waiting commuters, the younger ones of course. A number of the more elderly were disdainful but this didn't faze him. "Boring old farts," he thought to himself, "some people got no 'preciation." In fact their negativity only reinforced his pride in their achievement, underlined his sense of moral ascendency.

Shortly after the 8.13 pulled out he was joined by Tom and low and high-fives were again the order of the day, with whoops of joy and numerous "fucking amazing"s and "will you'se just look at that"s. The Captain was indeed a splendid sight, the colours of his uniform blazed in the daylight and his shield with its central white star, so difficult to render on such a corrugated surface, was perfectly round and symmetrical. Elated, the boys left to join the other prospective school-leavers. Not for them the throwing of laced together sneakers to hang forlornly from telegraph lines for a few weeks. No, they had created an enduring memento of their friendship and an expression of what they saw as their streetwise 'kultchure'.

The last week of school passed interminably slowly, but there was no point in bunking off, for the whole idle summer lay stretched out before them, or so at least they had thought. Schoolies' week was more for the academically gifted, the swots who had sweated revising for exams, those who were bound for more years of boring education, mostly at their parents' expense. No, as far as the lads were concerned they would be free, and there was plenty of time. What to do next could be thought of at leisure as they fished, and swam, and frolicked about. They were wrong. Disaster soon struck them a two-handed blow.

The first was a shock to them both. In the evenings going home Jack would always stop off at the station to glance at their artwork. It filled him with pride to have made a contribution to the life of the Port. In a grand and glamorous way he had made an indelible mark.

It was no longer there! Had been totally erased! No doubt in response to some elderly commuter, a railways clean-up crew had come along and maliciously painted the whole thing out!

In tears back in Tom's room whence he had speedily returned Jack described the foul deed that had wiped out their presence, superimposing a sickly yellow patch that stood out from the rest of the weathered, dull surface like a suppurating wound or a blister on skin.

"The bastards," said Tom, "those boring old fuckers. What have they ever done for the world?"

"I bet it was old Pomeroy," replied Jack, "I heard him belly-aching the very first day, going on to another of the suits."

"Let's go and egg his house," from Tom, "make it so it stinks for weeks."

So they did. Which was fun, and served the bastard right, but came nowhere close to appeasing the pain that was felt in poor Jack's heart. A pain which only grew more intense over succeeding days.

The second blow was delivered by his friend himself. Again in his room Tom was trying to console him by showing him the photos he had loaded onto his computer.

"Nipped down there one day with the digital and took a few shots. Come out well, don't you reckon? Took them to put in my portfolio. I'll print you some copies."

"What good's a copy when the real thing has gone? And what the hell's a portfolio anyway?"

"A collection of artworks. All my sketches and drawings, photos of the best paintings that I done at school. The old man told me I should put one together when I was round there for my weekend visit one time. And you know what he did?"

"What?"

"He showed it to some bloke he knows runs this advertising agency. And the feller said I got talent and he give me a job."

"You got a job?"

"Start Monday in town. Have to catch the train in at first a'course but it shouldn't take long on the wages he's paying that I'll be able to get a car. Just think of that, my very own wheels, the places we can go to, the clubs we can visit."

Jack was grateful for that 'we'. He tried his very hardest to join in his friend's enthusiasm but inside he was crushed. It was not so much the car although he knew as the law stood that it would be at least a year before he would be able to be taken anywhere at night. No, it was the loss of his friend and the summer he'd thought they'd be spending together. More than that, too, he could see. Tom would be moving on; a good job, a car, the money. Not immediately, of course, there would still be weekends, except the ones that he spent at his father's in town, but gradually, inexorably, their relationship would fade and he would be left here in the Port, with his pushbike, no money, and no friend.

"I'll have to wear a suit. Imagine that, me in a frigging suit!"

15

"That's a stretch."

"The glamorous bank's taking me shopping Friday night. She's over the moon a'course; 'It'll be the making of you Tom, be polite, talk properly, don't mess it up.' Oh well, what can you do? There's mothers for you."

And so it went. Tom to town daily on the 8.13 and Jack to mope around, mostly in his room. Even the beach had lost its allure. There was no fun unless it was shared. Wendy was at a loss to know how to handle her now disconsolate son. She suggested he go with her on some of her jobs if only to get him out of the house. He just wasn't interested. He'd once had a bit of pride in the vegetable patch out the back, making a small contribution to the family budget, but that was now a thing of the past. He occasionally visited the little workshop he had made in the shed at the back of the garden, but he ignored all of the half-finished woodwork projects that he had had on the go. Just sat curled up in the overstuffed armchair he had rescued from the side of the road one hard-rubbish day, and stared into space, seeing nothing. He even declined to go with her to the pictures on Semaphore Road, once their Saturday evening treat. Mostly he just lay on the bed for hours in his room, or else sprawled on the couch watching mind-numbing telly. In desperation she finally applied, on his behalf, for a job delivering Messengers, the local free newspaper, so that he'd get out of the house at least one day a week. He didn't want to do it but by this time she had lost all patience, she'd screamed at him that it would give him a little bit of money at least, he could do it on the bike that she had sweated to buy for him, and that he was being an ungrateful little sod. She was fed up with seeing his long face all the time and he should damn well get himself together.

16

The vehemence of her attack shocked Jack and he reluctantly agreed to undertake the paper-round for a few hours of a Thursday night. He wasn't happy but as he cycled the streets casting papers over fences he began to formulate a plan for revenge. He still had the sack with the remainder of the paint cans stashed in a corner of the shed. His efforts at creating some beauty round the place had been deemed to be worthless, to be entirely unacceptable, had viciously, he thought, been expunged. Well bugger them all, he would go on a tagging spree, see how the bastards liked that.

He was contemptuous of the numerous illegible squiggles that he saw on his bike rounds and determined on something more personal and, as Tom would have said, 'more artistic'. So he repaired to his shed and drew on a small bit of plywood the superimposed initials with which he had previously signed the Captain. Then with a drill and his fret saw he carefully cut round the outline, smoothing off any raised bits of torn grain with very fine emery paper. Now he had a stencil which he could hold on to any flat surface and with one deft sweep of an aerosol can, in seconds announce his presence in the world. The phantom would strike again and again.

He started with those houses he thought likeliest to have been the homes of complainers to the railways board, but soon extended his reach to any likely surface he fancied. He left the poorer dwellings alone, of course, he had no beef with the remnant old Portonians but there were not so many of the original families left. The increasing numbers of cafés and the variety of ethnically cuisined restaurants down Semaphore Road spoke of the changing demographic of the area.

He still saw Tom occasionally at weekends. His erstwhile companion had recognised the symbols appearing around the place and cautioned him against too much property damage.

"You don't want to be caught at it by the cops and end up doing community service."

"It *is* community service," he replied and Tom had laughed. He didn't understand.

Jack knew then that a gulf had widened between them. The job with its regular hours, the suit, the driving lessons from his mother had all contributed to the divergence of paths. Jack was left behind with the second hand bike which was now too small for him so that he began to feel ridiculous, with his knees coming nearly up to his chest as he pedalled. He missed the easy companionship of equals, the joint expeditions and the larking about. Although he wouldn't have been able to express it as such he felt that Tom was travelling a road towards the future whilst he was stuck back in the past; at the age of seventeen doing the job of a schoolboy, delivering newspapers to people who wouldn't normally have given him the time of day, who didn't even really see him.

The final straw came one Saturday night when he called round to see what his friend was up to. There was no reply and Jack was about to turn away when Tom's mother answered the door wearing a thin cotton dressing gown emblazoned with dragonflies picked out in red and in blue.

"Tom's at his father's this weekend, but come in for a moment, I've been wanting to have a private word with you."

Tom followed her down the hall and into her bedroom, staring at her stockinged calves which stretched alluringly from the hem of the gown to the pair of high-heeled, black shoes she was wearing.

"You'll have to excuse me, I'm getting ready to go out myself. You don't mind if I carry on do you?" as she turned her back on him and sat at her dressing table to continue applying her make up.

"N-no," Jack managed to reply, as he looked around at her boudoir; the cheval mirror standing in the corner, the framed Monet prints on the wall, the open wardrobe doors revealing rows of suits and dresses, the rack upon rack of her shoes, and lastly at her bed, across which was laid out a dress of black silk. He had never ventured into this room before and he was over-come with its opulence, so different from his mother's at home. Looking back at the cheval he found that he could see her, staring at her own reflection as she carefully applied mascara. The dressing gown had opened a little across her thighs and he could just glimpse the beginning of the dark band at the top of one stocking.

"There, that's done," as she laid down the wand and reached for a gold tube of lipstick. "Fire-engine red," as she manipulated the tube, "if this doesn't get him fired up then nothing will."

Once the fullness of her lips had been glossed and further emphasised with what Jack thought of as her war-paint, she pursed them together, parted them with a slight sucking noise and then turned to him and raised one arched eyebrow.

"Well, how do I look?"

"B-bloody f-fabulous," he stammered again, noting that as she had turned he could now see some whiteness at the top of one thigh.

"Why, thank you young man. A woman is never too old to receive a compliment, even if you *are* just being polite."

"I meant it," he expostulated, rather too forcefully, as she pulled the bottom of her dressing-gown closed.

"What I wanted to say is a little difficult for me, and I hope you won't take it the wrong way. You've been a good friend to Tom since we came out here to live, and believe me I'm grateful for that. When I think of some of the types...well, I'm sure you understand what I'm saying. It's just that I don't think you should call round for him quite so often. Now that he's got himself a good job in town he'll be mixing with other people, more his own sort. Tonight, for instance, he's going to a party with some of the others from the office, he's making new friends, and meeting new people. I don't want him to be held back. You do understand, don't you Jack?"

"Yeh, only too bloody well!" Deflated he turned and he fled from her room, slamming the front door in his haste to escape.

He ran all the way home and dived into the shed. Arming himself with his stencil and stashing a can of black paint into a plastic bag, he rushed back through the house, not bothering to answer Wendy's startled request, not even hearing it properly. He strode down Victoria Road as darkness fell, wondering what he should do. His thoughts kept returning to the 'glamorous bank' and the flash of her thigh that he'd been granted, heard again the rasp of her stockings as she had finally crossed her legs to address him.

On the Birkenhead Bridge he stopped and looked over, gazing at the dark waters below. A pod of dolphins was just passing through, maybe five or six, one a mother with a calf that played whilst the other ones fed, leaping straight up from the water to fall back with a splash, filled with energy at the pleasure of life, testing the strength and agility of its sleek young body.

"You lucky, lucky bastard," Jack thought and he crossed the road as they passed underneath him, and watched as they made their way downstream, making for the mangroves near the mouth of the estuary. Then raising his eyes he could see it – the lighthouse! Of course, that was the ideal place. The perfect edifice on which to inscribe his identity, from a great height his initials could glare down on the world.

The Port Adelaide lighthouse is a slender, red, cast-iron tube which flares out at the bottom to roof its few rooms, and is crowned by the curved white dome above the glass-walled lamp room, itself above an encircling railed platform. The whole is braced by a number of struts and girders, angling out downwards to be bolted to the ground. Over the years a number of boys have attempted to climb up the outside and once a car fleeing police in a high speed chase slammed full throttle into its side. 'They built things to last in the old days' people said, as the cast-iron structure suffered barely a scratch, but the car was totalled and the driver killed.

Jack slung the bag from one shoulder and began his ascent, first clambering onto the sloping metal roof at the bottom, then gingerly creeping, tightrope-walker style, up the angled cross-braces which prevented the main struts from flexing. At first he was nervous but the higher he climbed the closer the braces grew to the body of the structure and the nearer the hand-holds became. Finally he was just below the outflung platform and he paused for a moment to contemplate his next move. He had wanted to scale the thing right to the top, to place his insignia on the white of the roof, but was frustrated by the overhanging ledge. He thought wistfully of mountaineers with their karabiners and ropes, their metal pitons he had seen used on the telly, hammered into cracks above vertiginous heights. He decided that leaning out so precariously far, with only his fingers to support him, could easily result in a fall to his death and that was definitely not the aim of the exercise. It was life he was after, a glorious life.

So he unslung the bag from his shoulder and, crouching below the offending platform, he circled the tube, spraying over his stencil as he went. He placed his initials at each point of the compass, the four major and four minor ones as well. Then placated for the moment he carefully made his descent.

It was not quite enough to satisfy, however. Filled with elation as he was, from the safety of the ground his initials were lost in darkness, his triumph tempered by night. He moved off with other ideas fermenting in his brain.

Outside Tom's place he saw the house lay in darkness and the garage was empty, there was nobody home. Tom would be living it up at a party somewhere and his mother was out on her date. Since she had driven he reasoned she'd be staying the night, not brought back by her escort to disport in her own bed. He found the spare key in the hollow plastic log and let himself in, trembling the while. Her bedroom was at the back so he risked turning on the bedside lamp, figuring he would hear the car and the clang of the garage door should she return. Time enough to slip away with no one the wiser, whatever it was that he was going to do.

He surveyed the room, he sniffed at her dresses, he grasped for her pillow and inhaled. Turning to the dressing table he marvelled at her accoutrements, the myriad commodities of desire that were there displayed. He picked up each one of the bottles and jars, unstoppering them and breathing deeply at their contents, trying to inhale some essence that was her. He even went as far as turning out the lipstick and, remembering her lips flushed with 'fire-engine red', in a desire to taste them he delicately smoothed it around his own boyish mouth, puckered and sucked just as he had seen her do. With a hand now shaking he pulled open the top drawer to the left of the kneehole and there discovered her lingerie store. There her intimate apparel lay folded for his delectation, a profusion of colours, both pastel and bright, that set his mind to boiling. By now he had long lost all control. He reached his left hand in and buried it in silkiness, the fabric caressing his tentative fingers. Unable to withstand the surge of emotions that were now flooding into his adolescent brain, with his right hand he reached down and unzipped his fly.

THE CONSULTATION

I suppose you'll call it my mid-life crisis. Plenty of people did. Not my wife, God bless her, nor even my two sons, although I am sure they would have preferred me to buy something they could borrow at weekends; a low-slung red sports car for example. But, a petrol-head I emphatically am not.

My first car was an aged Morris Traveller, the model with the ash trim around the rear windows and doors, one previous owner; a careful, sedate and most reverend gentleman. In my estimation I have never owned a better designed and more attractive vehicle. I tell you this by way of explaining my character, so that you will better understand the decision that I made. I imagine you people reckon you can tell a lot from the kind of cars we drive.

Both Sandy and I were devastated when the wreckers finally came for Boris, for he was the conveyance of our courtship and of our early married years. Both sets of parents were insistent, however, that the imminent arrival of our first-born necessitated the purchase of something more reliable, something that would not break down should an emergency dash to hospital be required. Given that they were prepared to back their arguments with cold hard cash we had no choice but to acquiesce. So it was farewell to the intoxicating aroma of real leather upholstery when the sun shone brightly, as well as to the mushrooms that sprouted, whenever it rained, from the material on which the rear passenger windows slid. Regretfully we entered the era of Japanese design.

No, not my family, rather it was my work-mates who thought me crazy when I decided to give up my position at Consolidated Joineries and enrol in a degree course at university. When the monstrous howl from the mixed choir of woodworking machines fell silent at morning smoko, allowing the dust to briefly settle, and I announced my imminent departure to the tea room at large there was universal incomprehension, succinctly expressed by Colin as "English Literature, why the fuck?"

"Language," immediately shouted Rose, our tea lady, the only woman in the room full of thirty or so joiners, apprentices and process workers. Rose considered herself too much of a lady to countenance the use of the F-word in her presence, although she was very free with "bugger" herself. One day, upset at being told off once too often, I asked her if she knew what a bugger was. She looked around at the other people at our table with a wary look on her face and said "well, you know, stupid, like, an idiot." It was unkind of me I suppose to embarrass her so publicly, but I had been working on the overhead router for two days, the most dangerous machine in my area, moulding imitation panels onto full-length pantry doors, and she was one irritant too many. I just couldn't resist. "It's someone who fucks people in the arse." You can imagine the reaction.

After Colin's chastisement Bill moderated his comment to "he just wants to get his leg over some of those young student sheilas." Although spoken tongue in cheek, this was generally perceived as a perfectly acceptable reason for a forty-year-old man to want to go to university. Tea-room conversation usually revolved around either sex or what had been on television the night before, both if a particularly raunchy foreign film had been shown late on SBS. The Sex Before Sleep channel.

Having laughed off a certain amount of well-intentioned ridicule before the whistle blew for the end of smoko, as I walked back to my station I was tapped on the shoulder by old Derek, he of the two missing finger tips. I was about to re-start the spindle moulder and was contemplating the pallet of hardwood cupboard door panels I was still to shape when he shouted "Good on you, son. Get out while you can still hold a pen," holding up his right hand and waggling his stumps before pulling on his paper face-mask, plugging his ears with the company issue foam rubber bungs, and returning to his workbench. Derek only had three more years to retirement. You don't see too many old joiners with the full complement of fingers. Lucky he's left-handed.

I confess I was apprehensive myself. Twenty-five years on the tools since the start of my apprenticeship, bench-hand joinery was all I ever knew. Not that there was much hand-work done any more. Big machines. Big expensive machines. So, as with other fields, consolidation was the name of the game. Big fish swallowed little fish, growing fat on the entrails of their competitors.

Quality is still important of course, quality of looks that is, but not longevity. And certainly not individuality. Machines just don't do that. Not the sort of machines I'm talking about. The latest one in our factory cost over a million dollars. It has two saws which work at right angles to each other, enabling it to cut sheets of melamine coated MDF into whatever size has been programmed into its computer. We're making, say, fifty Morgana kitchens that week. The computer knows how many sides, backs, bottoms of whatever size are required for that many units, estimates the most economical way of cutting up each sheet and tells the operator how many sheets of the varying thicknesses it needs to do the job. All he has to do is provide them and hit the "on" button.

Load in, load out.

Which hardly requires Colin to have done his four-year apprenticeship. The firm did send him to Germany for a week so that he could learn how to program its computer, and to give him practice in operating it. On his return mostly what he seemed to have learnt was the difference between lager and pilsner.

Communist? Me? Don't be stupid. Show me any system not based on exploitation. The rise of the proletariat? I look around but I can't see it. It's been a bloody long time since a train driver sat in Parliament.

So what's this all about? Just trying to show you why I applied to university.

No, I've always been a reader, ever since I was a little tacker. Young Adult Historical Fiction I guess they'd call it now. Adventure stories was how I saw it; Romans, Vikings, King Arthur and his Round Table, Pirates, Coral Island, Black Arrow, all that. Then later Sherlock Holmes, and Poe, Ruth Rendell and all those other crime writers, and then along came the Russians. Oh God, the Russians! One reading of *Crime and Punishment* and I was gone, swept away in a deluge of Dostoyevsky, swamped by Tolstoy, gutted by Gogol, Turgenev,

Lermontov, Chekhov. Against the tide of current practice I gave up the television and took up literature.

Sandy understood. She had her own concerns, the three f's: family, food and fashion. And there was still plenty of the fourth, believe me, our interests might have diverged but our relationship was solid. Besides which, in the clothes that she made on her fancy sewing machine, she remained a real stunner. We didn't bother with Foxtel in our house, she had a sewing room and I had a shed. A bit different from that of most blokes I grant you but hey, I did my carpentry at work thank you very much. As well as the obligatory bar fridge my shed had a carpet, a comfy chair, and bookcases. Then, when I enrolled, a desk and a laptop. The kids had the living room, with the telly and their computer games.

When you've got a degree it's a kind of a passport, isn't it? You go into some lawyer's or accountant's office, and they've got all these qualifications hanging up on the wall in neat black frames, all great big red wax seals on them, fancy coats of arms and beautiful signatures. Yes, like yours over there – This is to certify that Harold Green etc., etc. What's it actually saying? "I'm fucking smart. I can fix your problems." I sincerely hope you can, otherwise this is all a waste of time, isn't it?

Not that I wanted a passport as such, I wasn't trying to prove myself to anyone else, but to myself, yes. I wanted my very own stamp of approval. I guess you'd say I was lacking self-confidence. And where are you supposed to get it from when your job requires less and less skill, when you gradually become more and more just a beast of burden, just a so-called unit of labour? Out of a bottle? Illicit sex? Shopping? Watching stupid reality TV shows? Call that entertainment? You've got to be joking.

I joined this sort of book club run by the WEA. Literary appreciation class. Bloody good actually, I really enjoyed it. Probably what gave me the idea. But inevitably you get into conversations about what you do for a living, and there's always some middle management wanker who goes "you are so lucky to be actually making things with your hands."

Yeah, right, he earns five times what I do, works less hours, sits in a nice office with a pretty secretary bringing him coffee, doesn't have to clock off when he goes to the doctor, the dentist, even the bloody hairdresser if he feels like it, doesn't have to wear a face mask, ear plugs or safety glasses, doesn't get covered in shit on a daily basis, doesn't have to worry about losing the odd finger or two. I mean, Ok he might get bored occasionally, but he could have swapped at any time if he truly believed in the nobility of good honest labour. He didn't.

Yes, alright, I'm being unfair, I know I am. To each our own alienation. Sorry about the rant, I only packed in the fags again a couple of days ago. Patches? What's the point of them? It's the nicotine I'm addicted to, not the breathing in and out.

Do you get any freebies from the drug companies? Travel and accommodation to conferences in exotic locations? No free pens and stationery with Bayer written all over them? No frequent flyer points per hundred diazepam prescriptions given out?

Sorry. Back to me then. So, university. Best years of my life. Wasted on the young. All that bullshit. But seriously, nothing to do all day but read books and think about them. It was like I'd died and gone to Heaven. Paid to read. Unbelievable. Ok, not really free, I've got a hell of a HECS debt to pay back. Not like the fuckers who passed that particular piece of legislation. Probably trying to keep people like me out of the system again, didn't like rubbing shoulders with the hoi polio when they were there, don't want their daughters sleeping with degenerates. Being a member of the Young Liberals must have been so uncool in the seventies. People probably laughed. So...

English Literature. Man, what a gas. Some of the things that people have written, thought, dreamed up. Loved doing the Renaissance. Shakespeare, Ok, we all know he's brilliant, we've been told it over and over so we just kind of accept it as read, but the others are almost as good; Webster, Marlowe, Middleton, Kyd, I'd never read or seen anyone doing their stuff on the stage. Thomas Nashe's *The Unfortunate Traveller*. "Old excellent he was at a bone-ache." There's a line will stay with me forever.

Then there was the older stuff, medieval. Chaucer and so on. Difficult to read at first but the old bat, the tutor, steered us through it and after a while it becomes quite easy, if you put the time in. Funny woman, all holey cardigans and tweed skirts, bit of a moustache on her upper lip, wrinkled hands with liver spots. A blue-stocking maybe, isn't that the word? Some of the students, the young ones, referred to her as the wicked witch of the west. Because she made them read the stuff when they didn't really want to.

Oh well, their loss. 'Cos it's brilliant stuff. Makes you realise that people haven't really changed much in six hundred years. I reckon that was my favourite course. I mean I told you I read all about King Arthur as a child, now here I was, forty years old reading the original Malory version. And *Sir Gawain and the Green Knight*, I'd never read his story before. It's so cool. I even had some original thoughts about that one, about what

Gawain's actual sin was. If you haven't read it you wouldn't understand but the gist of it was that he deliberately avoided confession, just when he needed it most. Bit like me maybe, although here I am, talking to you. The tutor, the old wicked witch, wanted me to send my ideas off to some journal called *Notes and Queries*.

No, I didn't. She said I would have to do some research first, get in touch with a Catholic priest who would have a clearer conception of what sin meant in medieval days. It seemed quite obvious to me so that I couldn't really be bothered. Besides which there was Kat.

Who was Kat? Well, here we come to the crux of the problem. I fell in love with Kat. She was some kind of post-punk, or maybe a Goth, whatever, all black hair, thick mascara and Doc Marten boots, and a real tough, take no prisoners attitude. But really sweet underneath it all, it was all a kind of self-protection I think, because she was small and also quite shy. Me too, the first few days I spent at uni I never even took my jacket off.

Anyway by this time we were in third year and well over that initial shyness and I suddenly realised that not only was she beautiful but that I was in love with her. She was not as blown away by all this medieval stuff as I was but she was interested, she did actually read the books and entered into the discussions in our tute groups. There were plenty who didn't. I guess it started from there, the verbal jousting we used to do in discussion groups. Carrying on afterwards over coffee or beers in the uni bar. I really liked her and she kind of made it obvious that she was interested in me too. Don't think she'd ever met a real 'worker' before.

I was probably part of her rebellion, same as the way she looked. I bet her doctor father hated the tat she'd had done on her neck, and the piercing through her eyebrow. Truth be told so did I, although I never told her that. She really was beautiful, can't understand why they want to disfigure themselves like that. Thank God she didn't have one through her tongue, that's got to be the worst.

And that's kind of the point. She was only a year or two older than Robert, my eldest son. So no, I kissed her a couple of times, or rather she kissed me, but I never went to bed with her. Why not? It's not that I didn't want to. Jesus, kissing her was delicious. The skin of her face and hands so…velvet, so…her lips…exquisite. Made me feel like I was twenty again. That rush. That feeling like you're the king of the world, like your heart expands till it wants to burst through your chest wall and carry you up and away like some giant red balloon hovering over the streets of Paris. Do you know that old film? Well, it felt kind of like that. Just floating.

But you can't, can you? Not when you're forty-three, been married for twenty-odd years to someone you still love and have two sons still at home. Ok, I could have fucked her, she made it clear that she wanted to, more than clear actually, but that's not who I am, and not how I was feeling. I loved her, so I couldn't.

Up to that point I'd always thought that you could only love one person at a time, but it's not true. Love isn't exclusive, is it? I love my sons, I still loved Sandy but a normal, quiet kind of love. With Kat it was gut-wrenching. Tearing. Painful. Like I could die. Like I was an adolescent again. Yeah, that's it, it was like I was a teenager again, with all that angst, and fear, and longing, like some kind of demonic possession.

So, what to do? I decided to wait it out. I remembered when I was a kid I fell in love with this girl from the tennis club. I was fourteen probably, she was a couple of years older, and not in the least interested in a pimply kid. I'd got it really bad though, followed her home once to find out where she lived, and then hung around her street for a couple of weeks, just on the off-chance of seeing her. But nothing happened and after a few weeks the pain I was feeling went away. Like flowers, if you don't water them they wither. At least that's what I thought.

So I started to avoid her. God it was hard. When that course finished I found out what she was enrolling in next, and chose a different one. Stopped going to the uni bar. Took sandwiches and a flask of tea instead of frequenting the café. Threw myself even more into my work, only going into uni when I really had too, spent my time working in my shed. Crying, sometimes, quietly, in my shed.

Sandy noticed of course, how could she not? But was too sensible to question me much. I gave up smoking for the first time then, to give myself an excuse for my erratic behaviour. The family bought it, Andy even gave up in sympathy to help me out, which was a bloody good thing because he stayed off them even when I eventually relapsed.

Kat graduated at the end of that year, whereas they offered me another year to do honours. What do you call it, "displacement activity"?

I don't know, I guess she was kind of pissed off with me for avoiding her because on her last day she sought me out, tracked me down in the quiet study area in the library. She kissed me one last time, and pressed something into my hand "to remember me by" and, laughing, skipped away. Stunned, I looked down at my hand and saw that she had presented me with a pair of the daintiest white lace knickers that I had ever seen. Something that a bride might wear on her wedding day. And they were warm.

Trouble is I just can't forget her. Even now, three years later. It wasn't like before, the pain never went away. I see her, now and again, walking through town, minus the eyebrow ring, pushing a baby in a stroller. Married a doctor, of course. Looks at me with a sort of wistful look in her eyes, says a word or two about the glories of medieval romance. And I laugh and wish her well, and don't tell her that I'm now on the dole, although she must realise that I didn't go back to being a bench-hand joiner. Otherwise I wouldn't have all this time to wander around the streets, or to consult with a psychologist.

ASHES

It had been a shit day, so after work I went with Dave to the Commercial for a couple of beers. I don't often go with him but I was really pissed off. Ultimately, as guides in the Maritime Museum we are public servants, however lowly, so in our way we are government representatives. Powerless ones but still…

The day had started usually enough. We let ourselves in through the aquamarine doors and while Dave counted the float into the till and logged on to check which school groups were due to arrive, I moved through the 1850s heritage building carrying remotes to turn on the several screens, projectors and soundscapes variously situated throughout all three floors.

Entering the silent and dimly lit museum is always a little eerie. The rows of ships' figureheads loom overhead, leaning out from the bluestone walls like a race of petrified giants, the ancient Baltic pine floorboards creak underfoot and in the basement the steerage bunks of the mocked up 1840s cabin with their hessian palliasses have a ghostly presence. The distraught looking female mannequin with the wild eyes doesn't help, lying there clutching her dead and sail-cloth wrapped baby tightly to her chest, too terrified to sleep lest someone snatch it from her for burial at sea.

Even when properly lit many of our younger visitors refer to the basement as a dungeon, and spend very little time down there. For our older visitors this is often the most interesting floor. There are numerous artefacts relating to the early settlement of South Australia: a large black rock which Matthew Flinders had carved his name into, various 19th century navigational instruments, and a ship's surgeon's tool kit with its grotesque bone saws, pincers and other accoutrements deemed necessary for a four month voyage in a crowded sailing vessel journeying half way around the world.

As well as the 1840s cabin there is one from 1910 and another from the 1950s. Once I have been into the control room and switched on the remaining lights and the CD players, each cabin comes alive with diary recitations of various immigrant voyages, played to background soundscapes of storms at sea, groaning timbers, creaking ropes or engine noises as appropriate.

There is much talk of death and disease in some of the earliest diaries, especially of the voyage of "that horrid ship, the Java", where scarlet and other fevers had stalked at will through the dim light beneath battened down storm hatches, liquidating without grace or favour both young and old. It's impossible to picture the abject poverty and starvation that had driven these intrepid travellers to venture into the unknown, many from my home county of Cornwall abandoning their outworked mines, or Irish farm labourers escaping blighted crops.

The 1910 diaries are more hopeful, reflecting increased safety and the leisurely atmosphere of a steam powered ocean cruise, recounting as they do the hopes and aspirations of young men and women expecting to set themselves up more comfortably in the colonies.

The diaries from the late forties and fifties return to a more sombre tone, narrating in various European accents peoples escaping the nightmare wreckage of the aftermath of war.

Economic migrants one and all.

Returning to the front desk I am greeted by Caitlin in broad Glaswegian before she makes her way down to our hundred and fifty year old lighthouse. When unmanned computer controlled beacons supplanted lighthouses it had been relocated from South Neptune Island to stand on the wharf, a proud symbol of the welcome once extended to arriving ships. Climbing its winding staircase to walk around the platform, just below the lamp-room, and gaze across town to the hazy promise of distant hills is one of the highlights for schoolchildren.

The museum depends for its finances on school excursions. It is no surprise that the younger ones prefer the ground floor where they can play on the full size replica ketch, which they all imagine as a pirate ship and act accordingly, turning the ship's wheel, climbing down into the holds and fighting mock battles with much crying of "aye, aye captain" and "avast, ye landlubbers!" When this tires they watch the film of dolphins in the Port River or, upstairs, roll balls down the throats of the beachside fairground clowns, practice surfing on the spring mounted board, play with various other inter-actives, or wonder at the exquisite scale model vessels displayed in glass cases throughout the museum.

Secondary school students, like the ones who arrived just after we opened, are treated to a more serious experience. The indomitable Alex Mann, volunteer extraordinaire, with two of his ex-wharfie mates, turned up to explain the importance of the ketches of the so-called mosquito fleet to the early economy of the state. These small vessels once plied their way up and down the gulfs picking up sacks of grain and bales of wool at the various jetties, bringing them back to the port for transhipment to the giant ocean-going clippers.

Alex is not so much a character as a force of nature. At eighty plus, a veteran of the wharves, ex-Federation vigilance officer and still leading light of the local diminutive communist party, his hearing damaged but short solid body toughened by a lifetime of hard physical labour, he whistles and sings as he waits for his charges to settle in front of him, and then explains that a child as young as themselves would have worked these vessels in company with the skipper. He encourages them to imagine the life of a fourteen year old in times gone by before inviting them aboard in small groups to try it for themselves.

This is when the other two, Smokey Bob and Wincher Bill, get the kids unwinding ropes from belaying pins and raising and lowering the heavy canvas sails. Having performed this task another group is positioned at different ropes to lift a fifty pound sack of grain utilising the wooden derrick, swinging it aboard and lowering it into the hold. The next group reverses the process.

Initially the students are fairly tentative; Smokey Bob reeks of cigarettes whilst Wincher can only mumble, as half of his tongue has been sacrificed to the ravages of cancer. Besides, all three old men are relics from a class and an era so unfamiliar to most of these clean cut kids that they might just as well have been ghosts themselves. The joy of the physical activity however, so different to their normal classroom routine, soon has them hooked, and when Alex tells them how many similar weighted sacks they had each carried on their backs in the course of their normal working day, the admiration glows on their faces. The more thoughtful contemplate how tough life must have been a mere forty or fifty years ago let alone way back when the ketches were operating. No amount of pretty speeches or words on a page can accurately convey the harshness of some people's lives.

Having delivered this program to each of three school groups the old boys came back to the desk to shoot the breeze for a few minutes. Alex in particular always enjoys a conversation, with a bit of a laugh and a joke. Lifetime political activist as he is, I always find his take on recent news illuminating. He is currently exercised about the treatment of illegal boat arrivals.

"So-called illegals," he spat out contemptuously. "Nothing illegal about it. Refugees is what they are, pure and simple. I know my George bloody Orwell; politicians always bend the truth by perverting the language, the slimy bastards. I never thought I'd live to see the day when we were locking little kiddies up in concentration camps. Bloody disgraceful, makes a man ashamed to call himself Australian. What about you Dave, what do you reckon on it?"

We have discussed this issue before and Alex knows exactly where I stand, so in true dialectical spirit he posed his question to Dave, purposely putting him on the spot.

Now I like Dave as a person, he's not the sharpest knife in the drawer, but he'll do anything for a mate if he can. Numerous times he has helped me out when I've needed some heavy lifting done at home or driven out of his way if my car's been playing up. But, you'd have to call him somewhat gullible, or perhaps just apathetic. All he wants is a quiet life. He's only ever voted Labor because he's a worker and that's what you do. He knows that the other lot are only concerned with reducing his pay and conditions, helping their mates live the high-life that he can only gaze at through the window of his television set, whilst he dreams on about winning the Lotto. On the other hand he has no time for 'dole bludgers' and other assorted parasites living off the taxes that he has paid all his life, and he is pretty sure that 'illegal immigrants' fall into this category. Welfare recipients in training. It doesn't help that many of them are Muslims. Whilst not religious himself Hollywood has brainwashed him with the idea that Islam is somehow 'barbaric'.

It is views like these that stop me drinking with him too often. I find it easier not to engage him in philosophical discussion. Not so Alex, of course. After a lifetime of practice raising the political consciousness of his fellow workers he just can't resist a challenge. I left them to it and went off to patrol the museum.

By the time I returned, having picked up several lolly wrappers, told a number of over-enthusiastic young boys to stop running, and answered the questions of a visiting Canadian couple in their seventies about the encounter between Baudin and Flinders off the coast near Kangaroo Island, Alex was just about to leave for the home that he had built some forty years ago, with the help of his mates and some 'damaged' building supplies from off the docks.

"Got a batch of home brew in the shed just come good," he said, "and the boys here reckon they need to check it for quality control. Then I've got to get me onions in."

I could just picture the three of them sitting around on crates in his garage, occasionally lifting a long-neck to their cracked and wrinkled lips, punctuating reminiscences of past actions or remembering old comrades already passed on into history. I thought how lucky the schoolchildren were to have such characters still around, volunteering what time was left to them to help with their education. And, as I watched them go, I realised I was jealous of their easy camaraderie. Work on the wharves before containerisation would have been tougher than I could stand. In my present condition I wouldn't have lasted five minutes. Still, I guess if I had been born here in the thirties or forties, like them I would have had little choice; toughen up or go to the wall.

At two o'clock all school parties left and I started on my rounds with a cloth and a bottle of Windex, wiping greasy fingerprints off our multitude of glass and acrylic surfaces. Children do so love to touch things, and if they can't handle the objects themselves then they reach out to get as close as possible. An hour later I returned to the desk to find Dave trying to cope with a group which had not appeared on the day's roster.

It is not unusual for us to host classes from the various colleges that teach English as a second language. Judging by the twenty or so young adults of differing colours and ethnicities, this is what I assumed this group to be. Such students usually pay individually the reduced group rate but in this case one of their three carers stated that he would pay for the lot. So, I welcomed them, explained the lay-out and the whereabouts of toilet facilities, whereupon three of the head-scarfed young women headed in that direction. The remainder filed into the body of the place, accompanied by the man and woman I had assumed were their teachers. It hadn't occurred to me until they had passed through the internal glass doors that these two were dressed identically to the remaining man who was handing a credit card to Dave. Blue short-sleeved shirts and trousers, thick leather belts with radios and other equipment suspended from them. A similar uniform to our own in fact, but without the tags displaying first names that were pinned to our chests. They had official looking identity cards, like driving licences, dangling from lanyards.

I studied the man as Dave completed the transaction and proffered his receipt. He was a big burly fellow with close cropped dark hair and what appeared to be a tattoo disappearing below his shirt collar, another on his left bicep. He looked for all the world like a night-club bouncer. Suddenly I realised what was going on. My suspicions were confirmed when he asked whether this was the only way out and Dave told him about the fire escape at the back.

"Is it alarmed?" he asked and got straight onto his radio to inform his two colleagues. We confirmed that it was and that yes, you could hear the alarm throughout the building. The three young Muslim women emerged from the ladies and he made several gestures shooing them after the others of their party.

"Think I'll stop here," he said "we'll only be an hour then the bus'll take us back."

"To Inverbrackie," I said.

"S'right. They get let out every now and again. Do the odd trip like this."

He was talking as if they were animals from a zoo, being given a bit of exercise.

"Manager says it's for their mental health. Don't want them sewing their lips together or any of that shit they do."

"Or riots," I say.

"Yeah. Although can't say I'd mind. It'd relieve the bore-dom, cracking a few heads."

"What's the pay like?" asked Dave.

"Not bad, long hours but. Why? You interested?"

"Nah, too far away. Takes me five minutes to get here in the mornings. Take about an hour and a half to get up there, I reckon."

I left them to it, went back inside. The refugees were having fun exploring the place, albeit under close supervision, playing with the inter-actives upstairs or climbing into the bunks down in the basement. A couple of the young women were standing stock still, staring aghast at the bereaved mother. I quietly moved away when I noticed that one of them had tears slowly running down her cheeks which her friend was wiping at with the ends of her headscarf.

I went back up to the ketch which a group of young men were admiring. One of them had a rudimentary command of English so with a few simple words which he translated to his friends and with a lot of hand gestures I got them untying ropes and lowering and raising the sails again. When this was done they all turned to me with broad grins on their faces. Their spokesman told me that his name was Abdul and he shook my hand and thanked me effusively for his help.

"Very nice boat, sir. Very…how you say? Be good in water."

"Seaworthy."

"Seaworthy, yes, thank you sir, very seaworthy yes."

The guard at the front desk blew a whistle and they all gathered for their trip back to the wire fenced enclosure in the distant hills, after he had done his headcount, of course. They smiled at Dave and I, every last one of them. There were numerous "Thank you, sirs," and not a few "As Salaam Alaikums." Peace be unto you.

Peace be unto you indeed.

After that I needed a drink.

There are several nineteenth century pubs still active in the Port's square mile. Some of them have been gentrified, selling boutique beers and the like, others have been completely refurbished behind their original facades with chrome and leather barstools and sofas, and hung about with abstract paintings of dubious quality. Still others cater almost exclusively to the dining trade. The Commercial has obstinately remained a working man's pub, serving pretty much the same type of clientele as when it was first built, sometime in the 1850s. Not so many sailors, of course, as when the Port River was choked with vessels, and the rooms upstairs were hired out, often by the hour. Nowadays the drinkers are mostly manual labourers and all kinds of tradespeople, standing at the long bar early in the morning, some of them, when their night shifts are over. Most people drift away for their evening meal not so very long after they would have done in the days of the six o'clock swill.

It being a Thursday the pub was packed, noisy with laughter and the odd heated argument. Television screens attached high on walls at either end were showing various horse racing meets and the TAB counter was doing steady business, its constantly ringing till adding to the general cacophony. Another screen was tuned to Foxtel, broadcasting the current Ashes test, which occasioned the odd cry or blasphemy from Elvis, the retired carpenter standing next to me.

I shouted us the first two beers as Dave launched into a prolonged rigmarole about the chances of the latest hopeful winning one of those interminable television talent shows that had been on the previous night. He watches such programmes religiously. When I evinced little interest he tried to drag Kate, the harassed looking bleached-blonde barmaid, into the conversation. Serving flat tack as she was, she could only reply with nods of the head and the odd brief comment as she reached into the freezer for cold glasses, or popped the tab on yet another can. Paul, at her side, wiped sweat from his eyes as he disgorged a steady stream of pressurised beer from the row of dripping taps. A couple of guys manoeuvred their way around the snooker table down by the toilets, with the press of the crowd making it difficult for them to line up their shots and Pat, with his battered old flat black cap perched atop his luxuriant grey hair, wove through the crowd, trying to look inconspicuous as he attempted to interest punters in his little Ziploc bags of grass.

Our first beers hardly touched the sides so Dave quickly set us up with another couple. Not wanting to get dragged back into a conversation about television, I stupidly asked him how he had got on with Alex.

"He got you joining the party yet?"

"Jesus, can he ever talk. And it's so bloody unfair. I mean I came out here with my olds when I was four, from Holland. So I know what it's like. We were real refugees, for God's sake. We wanted to fit in, find a new life. Not like some of these Somalis and Iraqis and suchlike. They just want a free ride. They're not like us. Different cultures, different religions, they don't try to fit in, do they? They want us to be like them."

Jack, a tall blond-haired welder, with ingrained blackened hands standing to Dave's left joined in.

"Too bloody right, mate. Fact is the country's full as it is. Where's the bloody water supposed to come from, that's what I want to know?"

Oh God. In desperation I turned to my right just in time to catch, above a sea of heads, an English wicket falling, and hear Elvis say, "That's the bloody way."

"Beaut piece of bowling, Elvis." Hoping to engage him in a more neutral topic of conversation.

"Yeah, but for how much longer?" He turned and jabbed a bent, arthritic finger at me.

"How do you mean?"

"You seen those new houses they've just built down Mead Street? They tore down five 'cos they was built on contaminated ground. Used to be a servo back in the day. And now they've put up fifteen on the same patch of land."

"So?"

"Well, kids can't play in the street like when I was a nipper can they? And those houses got about three feet to the back fence. Not a bloody hope of backyard cricket is there? So where the kids gonna learn? Those bloody poms are gonna *own* the sodding Ashes in a few years, I reckon."

I placed my beer glass sideways down on the bar and pushed my way through the heaving crowd to the doorway. I tried to shout goodbye to Dave but there was no way that he could hear me over the bedlam. "As Salaam Alaikum," I spoke softly to the room in general, then stepped outside.

The pavement was almost as crowded as the bar, with a throng of dedicated smokers leaning against the wall or sitting on the benches, all puffing away. Pat detached himself from the group he had just been transacting a bit of business with and approached me.

"What's up with you? You look right pee'd off."

"Bread and circuses, mate."

"Come again?"

"Beer and telly. All that. Sackcloth and ashes."

"You're fucking weird, you are. Always have been, ever since you went to university. Still, I got the perfect answer for you. Have one of these," reaching into his pocket for a bag, "that'll sort you out."

"Oh sod it, why the bloody hell not?" I paid him his twenty-five bucks and went for a walk down by the river.

ENTRANCE AND EXITS

A bridge is a structure loaded with symbolic overtones. So his father, a retired professor of English Literature, would say. A liminal place, suspended, as it were, between arrivals and departures, between entrances and exits.

On this particular cold winter's morning, as he gripped its railing, to Detective Inspector Martin Camp the Birkenhead Bridge was merely a vantage point, a platform for observation. He stared down at the steel grey waters which reflected the low sheet of cloud hammered to the sky above him. Under his black leather gloves his knuckles were white. "Would it be her?" he wondered.

He watched the rubber dingy of the police diving team slowly approach an oblong form wrapped in black plastic, with a bright orange life preserver attached to one end. He was his father's son: the irony was not lost on him.

To his left, as he looked downstream, were moored four of the port authority's tugs, one of whose massive diesel engines had probably disturbed the package, causing it to separate from whatever had been used to weight it down.

On the other side of the river, just below the wharf which housed the Fisherman's Market and beyond that the bright red exclamation mark of the Port Adelaide lighthouse, was moored the *Archie Badenoch*. It was a further irony that it should have been this ex-police motor launch, now owned and operated by the Maritime Museum, that had discovered what would probably prove to be a body, thus uncovering a murder. For murder it must have been. No suicide, however driven by despair to whatever ingenious lengths, could wrap themselves in black garbage bags, tape them together and then weigh themselves down.

The retired old wooden-hulled vessel was used by the museum to take parties of schoolchildren out upon the Port River. A rotating roster of skippers and crew, themselves retired seamen, would pilot excited youngsters up and down the deep waters of the still commercial estuary, in hopes of spotting members of the dolphin pod whose home it had been, presumably for generations. These sleek and elegantly playful creatures, having survived the increasing industrial pollution of the early twentieth century, were now making a comeback since containerization had moved most of the heavy traffic further downstream to the Outer Harbour. Sure, they still had to contend with cement dust spilling from the loading at the Adelaide Brighton Cement works, who knows what effluent from the soda ash processing plant, and over-heated water discharged from the Torrens Island power station. Spillage from the loading dock by the giant white grain silos was probably a plus, encouraging fish stocks, many species of which used the more sheltered waters of the estuary as a spawning ground, hence becoming food for the bottle-nosed dolphins.

The *Archie* was equipped with a hydrophone which, when lowered into the water near a dolphin sighting, would pick up the clicks and whistles of their secret language. Stuart, the current skipper, sometimes imagined it along the lines of "No fish here let's go upstream a bit" or "Man that little boat's really pissing me off."

49

In the current instance Stuart had fantasised the conversation going something like "Thank God, the smelly thing has broken free at last," and "Maybe the humans will get rid of it now." This after he had killed the engine and brought the object alongside with the aid of a boat-hook. Then, having caught the stench of decay emanating from the torn bin bags, he had leaned down and wrapped a life preserver around one end to keep it in plain sight, before heading back to his mooring to disembark his curious and excited passengers. Refusing to answer their questions, he advised their schoolteacher to take them straight back to the museum, before contacting the local police station with his suspicions about what the bundle might prove to be.

The Port Adelaide station had immediately put the wheels in motion, eventuating in the police diving team's rib being launched, and a forensics team and a number of officers standing about on the pontoon awaiting its return with its possibly grisly cargo. Martin was not based at the Port but had been phoned by one of its officers with news of the find. The whole force was aware of his obsession with dead bodies, so much so that he had earned himself the nickname The Ghoul. Whenever a body was discovered someone was bound to unofficially inform him. Later he would invariably turn up at the scene whether it was in his area or not. Very few of them knew the reason for this morbid fascination however. True, he was a Serious Crimes Officer and many of the cases following on from such a discovery would end up on his desk anyhow, it just struck the junior officers that he seemed somewhat distastefully 'over-keen'.

This was why he was now observing operations from the Birkenhead Bridge, having driven hell for leather from the centre of Adelaide. He couldn't intrude too early into the operation unfolding down on the pontoon, thereby alienating the local force. But he was desperate to find out if it was a body, rather than just some old collection of rubbish which had been thrown over the side of a departing merchant ship. And if it did indeed turn out to be a corpse, he was keen to ascertain its sex as soon as possible.

The rib had now reached the wharf and a multitude of gloved hands reached down to haul the package strapped to its side out of the water and onto the pontoon. The rib then made its way back out to the orange marker buoy with which the team had marked the spot. Martin watched as two divers gently slipped backwards into the water. He traced their movements by the beams of their high powered torches gradually descending the twelve metres or so, to search the estuary's muddy bottom for whatever they might find.

His attention returned to the pontoon where the booted, suited and face-masked chief forensics officer was slitting the black plastic with a knife and carefully laying it out, like a shy child at Christmas, on either side of what had once upon a time been a living, breathing human being. Martin groaned. So too did the police officers on the pontoon as they tried to distance themselves as far as possible upwind of the bloated carcase thus exposed, leaving the field clear for the hardened forensics officers breathing through their scented face masks to take their photographs, probe whatever clothing remained, and take the multitude of samples required. It hardly seemed necessary for the doctor to pronounce death, and Martin could see that the pathologist was already engaged in argument with the Chief Investigating Officer, no doubt telling him, somewhat forcefully, that there was not a hope in hell of giving a time of death until she had carried out the post mortem. It was time for Martin to move. He had to see the body before the coroner's people removed it to the morgue.

He climbed through the hole in the fence at the end of the bridge and descended to the concrete floating pontoon down a metal ramp covered in blue anti-slip material. Approaching Bill Masterton, the CIO from the Port Division, he nodded a greeting and looked towards the body.

"Mind if I take a look?"

"Fill your boots." Said with a grimace.

Covering his nose and mouth with a handkerchief Martin stared down at the partially decomposed body of a woman, hands and feet gaffer taped together and with a large section of the back of her skull staved in. The wrists had been taped in such a way that the hands were palm to palm in the prayer position and placed on her chest. He turned and started to walk away.

"Seen enough, have you?" Bill asked, a distasteful curl to his upper lip.

"I'll tell you this for nothing," he retorted, "he loved her, the stupid bastard who did this."

"What makes you so sure it was a man?" Bill sneered.

"Isn't it always?" Martin shot back as he left the scene.

He felt angry, disappointed but relieved all at once as he made his way back up to the bridge. Viewing the corpses never got any easier, he always came away with this confused mixture of emotions. He tore off a glove and reached into his jacket pocket for his phone. He stabbed out his father's number and on getting a response, merely whispered, "Some poor woman, but no, it's not her."

MIRROR MAN

Frank McKenzie was worried. Staring into the mirror above the sink in the en-suite bathroom, copied from a magazine by his thirty-one year old wife, he examined his face with a degree of fastidiousness unusual for him. Staring back was a face reversed in polarity from that observed by everyone else. Since childhood he had considered that only he could see it truly; his left as left, his right as right. Mirrors had always held a fascination for him and eventually they had become his business.

To the left of his substantial nose, with its smattering of fine, near-invisible hairs riding its spine towards the more pronounced ones sprouting from both nostrils, and half way across his fleshy cheek towards the similarly endowed left ear-hole was a feature previously unobserved; a tiny spot. No, not a spot exactly, for it was not raised above the plane of skin that had enclosed his face adequately for some fifty-six years. Moreover it was miniscule, not an eruption as such, more like a blocked pore, a sealed entrance to the subcutaneous world beneath his face.

Normally this would have not have troubled him. Although long past adolescence, occasionally he still played host to the odd blackhead which he took a secret pleasure in squeezing, delighting in watching the congealed yellow globule of fat beneath its black hat slowly emerge or, more satisfying still, a writhing, wrinkled, thin white snake suddenly bursting forth, as if striking out at some invisible prey. No, blackheads were no threat to him but this miniature trap-door was red, and caused him to remember the news story that his wife had regaled him with a few nights previously.

One of the country's biggest film-stars had disclosed, while making a speech accepting some award or other, that a small red blemish had appeared on his nose. A blemish so tiny that indeed he had not noticed it himself. It was only because of his exalted occupation, involving as it did daily ministrations by a team of hair stylists and make-up artists professionally involved with every nuance of his appearance, that it had been brought to his notice in the first place.

During the course of his oration the actor had revealed that it was only through the dogged insistence of his wife that he consult a medical practitioner, that the life-threatening nature of this minute defect had been discovered, and subsequently dealt with. And so he had thanked her profusely in this public address, and advised men everywhere to listen to their partners, and to overcome their reluctance to trouble their G.P.s with matters seemingly inconsequential. Frank wondered whether his own wife would be so concerned about this discovery of his. On balance he thought not. He decided to remain silent but to monitor this change in his appearance closely. After all he had far greater worries beavering away in his subconscious.

Firstly there was his wife, of course. Was she really having an affair with, presumably, a much younger man? For the past few months she seemed to have been spending an inordinate amount of time working out at her gym, or, alternatively having hit-outs at the tennis club. The unsought explanation of her determination, now that she had passed the age of thirty, to stave off any spreading effects of an impending middle-age, sounded reasonable enough. She was what is vulgarly termed a "trophy wife" after all, and they both knew it. Some few months after the death of his first wife she had graduated from secretarial work-mate to enthusiastic bed-mate and, a year later still, to marriage partner in a flamboyant and expensive ceremony of her own devising. She was merely keeping to her side of the bargain, she insisted, working to maintain her attractiveness for his benefit alone.

Doubts remained, however.

More pressing, during daylight hours, was the decision he had to make about the Japanese offer for his business. Tokyo had made it clear that they expected a response within a fortnight whether yea or nay. It was fairly obvious that they were confident of his acquiescence. Really, what choice did he have? He could either retire a rich man or watch the company, that he had so painstakingly built up over the years, fade into obscurity, along with all the other Australian car component manufacturers.

The problem was the responsibility he felt for his workers. If he sold up what would become of them? His foreman, Bill, had been with him since he had first established McKenzie Fabrications, housed in one of the disused cargo sheds that lined the Port River wharves. Many of the others had worked there for nearly as long. Indeed, without their hard work would the company be worth what the Japanese were prepared to pay for it? Ok, he could insist on a clause being inserted into the agreement that they would all be kept on in their present jobs, but for how long would that be honoured once the factory was theirs? He was under no illusion that they were actually after his business, his factory, or his workers. No, the prize in all this was the plastics moulding process that he had invented, enabling the construction of wing mirrors at half the standard cost. Once they had acquired that then they could set up their own factory in whatever cheap labour country that they fancied. Their cars were currently being built in South Korea, but Thailand was being favourably considered by many multi-nationals; peasants were flocking to the mega-cities of China; Bangladesh was always a possibility; Burma looked like opening up under its new name; and of course there was the joint economic zone in North Korea, just across the border from their present assembly plant. It wouldn't take long to train a new work-force, the process wasn't complicated; easy enough for prisoners, or starving people, or even, God forbid, for slaves.

Having completed his usual morning tour of the assembly lines, sharing the odd joke with this or that person, he sought out Bill to request the most powerful magnifying glass that the factory possessed. Oddly, for such an enterprise involved in precision optics he could only come up with one which had a disappointingly low magnification. He grasped it however and hurriedly disappeared into his executive bathroom. Holding it between his face and the mirror he sought to study the small red dot, without much success. Even when he had ransacked his desk and returned wearing his reading glasses the blemish was not much clearer, and the dimple of higher magnification inserted near the glass's base was totally useless, as to raise it high enough meant that his eyes were obscured. Frustrated he returned to his desk to consult his list of suppliers. He was about to order the highest magnification glass that could be delivered as swiftly as possible when he suddenly remembered the camera shop in town. He rapidly left the factory, advising Bill that he would not be gone for long.

His excitement rubbed off on his foreman. Having worked together for so long he thought that he recognised the signs of a new idea firing the imagination of his boss. Something that could lead to a new invention perhaps, and ultimately a product divorced from the automotive industry, which everyone could see was crumbling around them. He remembered Frank's feverish activity in the weeks before the prototype of their current product was unveiled; the late nights and weekends that the two of them had spent together perfecting its manufacturing process. They had been a team then, rather than employee and boss, and between them they had sweated and laboured, refined and polished and eventually brought their new product successfully to market.

Bill was only too aware that something had lately been troubling Frank. He had been lacking a certain bounce in his step, a certain energy of determination. It was as if his batteries were running low, or that the dynamo which normally fuelled his aura, like some electrical force field, was only running at half speed. To see his boss virtually running across the car park outside, throwing himself into his BMW and roaring off, spraying gravel as he went, he took to be a good sign, a renewal of enthusiasm and vigour. He mentioned his hopes to Mrs. Morrison, the middle-aged and rather dowdy secretary who had been selected by the new Mrs. McKenzie as her own replacement.

"He's had an idea Mrs. M. I reckon things might be looking up. Once he gets a thought in his head he worries at it like a terrier with a rat. It was like this with the wing mirrors and look where that got us. Oh yes, you mark my words, things are on the improve."

Half an hour later they watched as Frank returned as precipitately as he had left, and once he had disappeared into his office they speculated as to what might have been in the tiny parcel he had carried in with him.

Tearing open the package as he went, Frank moved through his office into his bathroom, scattering the torn wrapping paper on the floor to reveal his newly purchased loupe. Frustrated by the weakness of the magnifying glass he had suddenly remembered this little piece of equipment. It was something photographers use to study the small images on their proof-sheets, before selecting which ones to blow up to full size. It was a small black tube with a fixed lens at one end with a lower section of clear perspex to let in light. In his enthusiasm he firstly held it up to the mirror over the area where the reflection of his spot showed. Of course as soon as he tried to look down the tube he had to move his head and all that he saw was a greatly enlarged pupil staring right back at him. Reversing it he now held the base of the loupe against the skin of his cheek and moved his face forwards and backwards until he could see the reflection of the magnified blemish in proper focus.

It was not particularly satisfactory as his face was curved, not flat like a contact sheet, and moreover, as he breathed in and out, the focal length kept altering minutely and the moisture of his breath bouncing off the mirror tended to fog up the lens. Nevertheless he stood there for ten, fifteen, twenty minutes avidly studying the enlargement of a section of his face as he stared into what looked like a crater on the red planet when viewed through a telescope. He wasn't sure, but after a period of time he began to imagine that he could discern some minute movements within it. This unsettled him enough to immediately arrange an appointment with his G.P. for later that afternoon.

His visit to the surgery was a frustration and a disappointment. Firstly he had sat in the waiting room for nearly three quarters of an hour, whilst various snuffling children with their over-anxious mothers monopolised the doctor's time with what any fool could see were just minor complaints. Distaining to study the plethora of celebrity gossip magazines scattered around the place, all he had to take his mind off his present medical trouble was the contemplation of either his relationship or his fiscal problems, neither of which were guaranteed to calm him in the least.

On finally being ushered into the inner sanctum the doctor turned out to be a fool, totally disinterested in his condition. He did the usual routine of blood pressure cuff, stethoscope to the chest, peering into his ears, opening wide and saying "Aaah" and so forth, before he finally reached for his own totally inadequate magnifying glass and looked at the affected area for a couple of seconds. He pronounced it to be nothing more than a blocked pore.

When Frank informed him of the movements within that he had observed, the silly man only asked if he had been sleeping well recently. To this Frank was forced to reply that he had a lot on his mind. The upshot of this being that when he exited the surgery once his ten minutes were up, he carried in his hand a prescription for diazepam.

Rather than calling in at a chemist's, Frank drove straightaway back to the factory. There he again consulted his list of suppliers and spent a frenzied half hour ringing around and ordering microscopes, telescopes, prisms, mirrors both convex and concave in a variety of sizes, and all manner of other laboratory equipment to be couriered to the business without delay.

Having completed his transactions he drove home intent on quizzing his wife on what the film star had actually said about his disfigurement and what it had turned out to be. Her car was gone however, and there was a note on the hall table informing him that she was taking part in a mixed doubles tournament at the tennis club and that she wouldn't be home until late. Resisting the urge to phone the club, instead he ordered a take-away pizza before pouring himself a large scotch and retreating to his den to await its arrival.

He wondered who her partner might be, either in the supposed tournament or otherwise, and that brought him back to the Japanese question. If he sold, and he couldn't really see that he had any option but to do so, then he would suddenly be worth several million dollars. Enough to retire on perfectly happily, and possibly move up to Queensland to take up sailing or golf. But what would his wife do then? Divorce him and take half of what he had spent his lifetime earning? Probably, he thought, if she really was playing away. After all, why had she married him in the first place? Not for his looks, that was for sure. For his fascinating and engaging personality? He sincerely doubted it. She was an avid reader of romance novels, and he knew that these encompassed whole sub-genres of secretaries marrying their bosses, or nurses finally wedding surgeons and finding true happiness; but the men in these fables were all a lot younger than him, more virile than him, and a lot more handsome; ripped he believed the current term to be. No, he was under no illusions, it was simply about money, and it always had been.

The next day his parcels started arriving. Bill could barely contain his enthusiasm as courier van after courier van pulled into their car park. "Here comes another one Mrs. M.," he would shout, and smile and wink at her and add, "Oh yes, things are definitely on the improve." He was disappointed that Frank was not prepared to share with him however, merely emerging from his office to snatch each successive parcel from the hands of the surprised driver and disappearing with it back into his private domain, leaving his apologetic secretary to sign the delivery chits. Finally a dressing table arrived, much to the surprise of Bill and Mrs. Morrison, to be carried by the removal men into Frank's workshop to the far side of his office.

"What the hell?" thought Bill, and then wondered if a bed was soon to follow. He had known Frank's first wife and thought her to be a lovely woman, a tireless support to her husband, bringing him in supper when he was in the throes of a new invention, and always with a kind word to his workers or a genuinely interested question about their families. He was shocked when their glamorous but ditzy new secretary became his second wife and many times had discussed the potential longevity of the union with his own spouse. In silence he speculated that some trouble at home was the probable cause of Frank's recent lacklustre appearance.

The dressing table itself was an old 1940's style oak number with a large central mirror and a smaller adjustable wing to each side, designed for a woman to study the sides of her face as well as full frontally when applying her make-up. Once the removalists had placed it against the wall of his workshop Frank got them to move his workbench right up against it before slipping them the price of a few beers each. When they had gone he wheeled his office chair into the room and sat studying his face for a while. Then he started to work.

As well as the woodworking vice at one end, his bench was equipped with a number of small engineers' vices mounted along its surface. Into these he wound a number of metal arms surmounted by clamps which you might have found clasping beakers in a school chemistry lab. Instead of beakers however, they now gripped any manner of other paraphernalia, such as magnifying lenses or smaller reflectors which he had removed from the telescopes which lay in various stages of disassembly across the surface of his bench. From time to time he would rest from his feverish activity, to sit in his office chair and survey his handiwork, and then stare at his increasingly magnified face. At one point he leapt up muttering "light, light" and rushed back into his office to collect the anglepoise lamp from his desk and subsequently mount it on the bench. Still unhappy with the resultant lux level he ran through his office into Mrs. Morrison's domain to grab the one from her desk, as well as the free standing chrome armature surmounted by dual spots by the side of the visitors' couch. With all of these positioned to shine on his face he resumed his seat and studied the clarity and magnitude of his reflection.

This was much better and with his image bounced from one mirror to the next, and through any number of magnifying lenses, he was able to study the blemish blown up to such a scale that he was now clearly able to see that there really was movement occurring within it. A lot of movement. He returned to the piece of graph paper on his desk where he had roughly jotted down distances and angles and then back into the workshop with a tape measure to make adjustments to the clamps holding the plethora of prisms, mirrors and lenses that he had so far arranged. Better, he thought. The image now had a sense of depth, the delineation of an interior space wherein the movements were taking place.

His next trip was into the factory itself to collect some strips of steel and to load the portable welding gear onto a sack-truck. Bill, almost bursting with curiosity, offered to wheel it back for him but his offer was curtly refused. He was disappointed but not in any way offended, for it merely confirmed that his boss was on the verge of some break-through. He resumed his tour of the assembly line, sometimes slapping people on the back and complimenting others on the quality of their work.

Back in the workshop Frank started bending the metal strips and then welding them together until he had created a kind of a coronet with suspended flanges which he donned to check for fit and rigidity. This was then welded to the back of his chair, so that when he sat and closed it around him it would hold his head fixed in the appropriate position, allowing no possibility of movement.

Finally he unwrapped the last of his parcels, revealing a high-powered and very expensive microscope, which he immediately started butchering, tossing the unwanted elements onto the floor behind him. The base went first, followed by the little mirror and then the platform upon which the slides were supposed to be held, leaving him just the tube with its selection of lenses and the little adjustment wheels with which to bring objects into the sharpest of focus. This he clamped to a final armature, mounted in such a way that he could swing it in front of his eye once he was seated. This was the most crucial piece of his apparatus and he spent a great deal of time lining it up absolutely precisely so that the image captured in the dressing table mirror would be reflected via one of the wings into a series of prisms and lenses, and from one small mirror to the next, ultimately to arrive into the body of the microscope and from thence into the eye of the beholder held immovable by the steel carapace.

The moment of truth had finally arrived. Frank turned off the main lights and altered his selection of lamps to shine fully on his now re-designed designer office chair. Taking up his position as if solemnly mounting some futuristic throne, then crowning himself with the coronet of steel, he swung the microscope towards his left, his dominant eye. In this position he could easily reach the little wheels to wind the microscope in or out to bring the blemish into perfect focus, unobstructed by any intervening objects and magnified enormously.

His eye, or more properly his brain, took some time to decipher the image thus presented to him. It seemed as if he was staring into a cave, a cave filled with flickering shadows whose walls of flesh pulsed and throbbed. Gradually the shadows revealed themselves to be thrown by the tiny figures of men, who were attacking the walls with all manner of knives, and picks and shovels, for all the world as if they were flensing a whale. As they worked they threw the excavated flesh onto a wide conveyor belt circling in the middle of the cave, like the continuous baggage retrieval at an airport. With a gasp he realised that these small figures were the members of his own workforce, hacking away at his very substance. As if that were not enough, there, lying on the moving belt was the figure of his wife, lasciviously displaying herself, dress pulled up way above her breasts, her knees bent and thighs outstretched to accommodate the figure of Bill, who was gripping her shoulders from below, and pounding into her body with a virile frenzy unmatched by anything that Frank himself had managed to accomplish over the years in their marital bed. And as they circulated the fleshy grotto one by one men would turn from their butcherous task to whistle and cheer on the wanton couple, occasionally to slap Bill in celebration on his naked thrusting rump.

Frank let out a terrible wail, flung the microscope away from him and attempted to jump up from his cockpit, wrenching his neck in the process, having totally forgotten the steel bands that held his head prisoner. Hastening to unfasten the helmet-like structure he called out for Mrs. Morrison, who in fact had already entered the workshop, closely followed by Bill, running, as they had thought, to rescue him from some experiment gone horribly wrong. Confronted as they were by the sight of their boss struggling to extricate himself from a contraption which looked like a cross between an electric chair and a piece of apparatus from the laboratory of Doctor Frankenstein, the pair of them were totally dumbfounded. More so when, with a sour look on his face he rounded on his secretary and commanded her to "get me Tokyo on the line!"

THE WOMAN WITH
A PEARL EARRING

When Marguerite comes into the gallery I look forward to a good night. I don't know her very well but I like her a lot. She has a smile like a treasure chest opening, a beautiful soft voice, elegantly modulated, and absolutely exquisite manners. Especially to bar staff, such as myself; I am not so conceited as to believe it is just for me.

So often at exhibition openings I am treated by the invited freeloaders as some kind of a lackey. They look through you as if you were nothing but a wine vending machine in human form, some surrealist fantasy that Mike, one of the gallery's owners, has fabricated during one of his well-known attacks of whimsy (press the red button, press the white, or both of them together if you want hot chocolate). Or they just thrust their glass out in my general direction for a refill whilst continuing their weary chatter with some Justin, Julian or Samantha. There are few things as tiring as people droning on about art, trying to impress each other with their hip sensibilities. Real artists on the other hand are a different teapot of smoked fish. They boil with enthusiasm, their heads like pressure cookers approaching bursting point; they find it so difficult to express themselves in words.

Which is why they paint of course, or do whatever else it is that they do.

Tonight she has her silver hair tied up in a blue scarf, wears long drop earrings and a silver filigree brooch pinned to her orange jacket. She walks with a limp and clutches an ebony cane topped with a silver dog's head that would have made Salvador Dali weep. Does she have a few more lines etched into her ageing face? I think so, but at seventy you have to expect this, I guess. Her eyes though, those grey-green so-called mirrors of the soul, her eyes sparkle with expectant joy, just as they must have done when she was a young girl on the cusp of womanhood. Her eyes invite you to dance a pavane, whatever the hell that is, or perhaps I mean a gavotte. She makes her way tentatively around the room, giving each work a full five minutes of serious contemplation, before making her way over to my makeshift bar.

"The leg's new," I say, handing her the glass of Shiraz that I have poured ready for her.

"That's just the trouble, it's not. Banged my knee, look," and she reaches down and hoists her skirt a good six inches to reveal the thick binding of pressure bandaging.

"You old flirt, you," I say. "You're trying to distract me from my work."

"If I were only five years younger I'd make you work alright," she replies and we both crack up laughing. "Slipped over in the shower, banged it on the edge of the bath. Don't ever get old, young Edward, believe me it's a real bugger." I tell her to get one of those non-slip bath mat things.

"I'm going to need something more than that soon," she says, "like someone to do it all for me." I tell her that I'd volunteer willingly but that I'm afraid my girlfriend gets terribly jealous, and she'd probably do more than just bust her knee, and we both fall about. Well, not literally of course, Marguerite was obviously having a painful enough time of it just remaining upright.

"Care for a top up?" I ask.

"You're a wicked boy," she replies and hands me her glass.

She comes to all the exhibition openings and I've noticed that she is partial to more than a drop or two of red wine. Well, living as we do between the Barossa and Clare Valleys to the north, McLaren Vale to the south, the Adelaide Hills to the east and only the 'wine-dark' sea to the west, who wouldn't? Certainly not me. Our usual opening gambits involve an exchange of information about the various vintages we have tried, or vineyards that we currently favour. She once told me that after the death of her husband she doesn't get out so very much but that luckily she has friends who take her around to all of the openings.

That gave me pause for thought. I realised that although I hardly knew her I was a major part of her social life, so I started paying her more attention. I tend bar at all of Mike and Tony's gallery openings, as well as doing odd jobs for them around the place when required; hanging paintings or feeding their Siamese cats and watering pot-plants when they travel. So I see Marguerite maybe three or four times a year. She is always full of the kind of fun that only certain old ladies can dispense from their glory boxes of memories. She regales me with stories of places she has been, sights she has seen, like some latter-day Scheherazade. She met her husband when she was a cabaret singer working the cruise liner circuit in the sixties, and he was a steward for P&O. When her contracts ended she would often choose to disembark in some exotic port, travel for a month or so, and then sign on again catching the next ship through. "I was a sea-born gypsy me," she laughed, "until I was beached by love."

Tony has noticed the limp from across the room and, once his welcoming speech is over and he has introduced the artists whose works bedeck the walls like so many blown-up postage stamps from new nations, he threads his way through the throng.

"Dear lady," he expostulates when her accident is reported; he is such an old queen at times, standing there in his double-breasted navy blazer, slacks, and mustard cravat with matching top-pocket handkerchief. "Edward, I notice that all of our guests are holding glasses that are currently charged. Perhaps you would be so kind as to run upstairs to our apartment and retrieve a chair for dear Marguerite. Elegant as that cane is, my dear, I can't help feeling that something a tad more substantial would render you a greater degree of stability, not to mention comfort." He not only dresses as if he has just stepped out of the pages of an Edwardian novel, he talks like it too. For all that he has the kind of incisive business acumen that enables their joint enterprise to flourish (it is Mike who is the artist of the couple), Tony has a heart both burnished and pure. I don't recall Marguerite ever having bought a work from them, yet he treats her as if she were his most valued customer. I guess that's the kind of effortless humanity that she inspires in people. Grace, that's the word for it, grace bestowed which in turn invites reciprocation.

Ensconced in a reproduction Chippendale carver, with her cane lying across her thighs so that she looks like the presiding genius of some kind of Egyptian Bacchanal, as staged by D.W. Griffith, she says, "Tony is such a love. He was a great friend of my late husband Brian's." She notices my raised eyebrows. "Not like that, dirty boy. Brian might have been a sailor but he was as straight as a die. They met when we first moved here from Broome. I'll tell you if you like."

This was the first time I'd heard her make mention of Broome. It appears that when they had decided on a more land-based life-style they'd signed off in Perth but Brian had been unable to find work at first. So they'd moved up to Broome and he'd spent a couple of years working the pearl fleet up there. Deckhand and occasional diver.

"Bloody tough job," I say.

"Bloody tough life, living in a tin shack, no refrigeration, no air-con back then. Well, anyway, eventually we had ourselves a bit of luck so decided to travel round God's own for a while. We ended up down here. Saw it and liked it. Brian got himself a job on the Moonta, you know, pleasure cruises up and down the Gulf; two, three days away at most, so we stayed.

When Brian was coming back from the ship one night he came upon two thugs kicking the proverbial out of some poor man lying on the ground, just by the side of the wharf. They were young, big blokes but so was Brian. Two years working pearl luggers is better than a gym any day for keeping you in shape. So he whaled into them until they ran off, one with a bloody nose and the other who he reckoned would have sported a beautiful shiner the following morning. He stooped down and helped the groaning man to his feet, then sat him on a bollard. 'Want me to call the cops for you, mate? I'll be witness if you like. They steal anything?'

'No, no cops,' said Mike, for Mike it was. 'My fault, my fault entirely, no cops, thank you.'

'Oh,' says Brian, beginning to get the picture. 'Well, let's get you to the hospital then, they probably busted a rib or two and you might well have some concussion. You sure you don't want the cops though? It looked to me like they were aiming to roll you over the edge.'

'No, please, don't bother. And no hospital either. I'll be alright. I've had worse. Though never the offer of a watery grave,' and he attempted to stand, staggered and collapsed back down again.

'Well, you'll come home with me then, the missus'll fix you up a bit and then I'll drive you to your place.'

'Oh God,' groaned Mike, 'Tony's going to kill me.'

'Not after I tell him what I saw he won't.'

'You don't understand,' said Mike.

'I think I do mate, I think I've got a fairly shrewd idea.' With that he hauled the battered man to his feet and helped him towards our car. I fixed him up as best as I could, cleaned a few cuts, dispensed a few band-aids then Brian drove him here.

Tony was furious, of course, but Brian said that he had almost been murdered once that night, and that if he were to lay so much as a finger on the poor unfortunate then he'd have him to deal with, and that he'd be back in the morning to check.

'Wouldn't dream of it, dear boy,' a chagrined Tony said, 'but perhaps you'd help me get him upstairs and I'll put the poor love to bed.' Brian did go back, like he said, and although Tony was still angry, he was more than a little grateful for Brian's Good Samaritan act.

'That stupid little boy,' he said. 'He just can't help himself. Every now and again he just has to go out looking for adventures. Maybe this time he'll learn his lesson, but I fear the worst.'

Ever since that day Tony and Brian became the best of friends, and Mike too of course, although with him there always remained a vestigial shadow of, I don't know, embarrassment I suppose."

Part of my exhibition duties involves the day after clean up, so I was up to my elbows in soap suds when the phone rang – although we use it for plates and cutlery Tony won't hear of wine glasses going into the dishwasher, "Never get them properly clean, dear boy, nasty smears all over them. I wouldn't put them anywhere near my cherry reds and I wouldn't expect less for any of our guests."

"Oh, Edward, it's you," I recognise Marguerite's mellifluous tones. "Last night somewhere I lost an earring. It's really...um, it's quite valuable and it...er, it means an awful lot to me. I don't suppose you've come across it anywhere have you?"

I have never, ever, heard her stumble over her words before.

"I'm afraid not," I reply, "what does it look like?"

"You'd probably recognise it, I usually wear them. A silver drop with a rather large pearl. Brian had them made for me."

"I know the ones. Look, I haven't done the vacuuming yet. I'll have a really good search around and give you a ring if I find it."

"If you would be so kind. I'll be having lunch today at Anna's café, just around the corner from the gallery; perhaps you could drop it in there, should you find it, of course."

"Of course I will," I reply.

I lied. I have already done the vacuuming. And saw no earring. But I go out the back and empty the bag onto a sheet of A3 and go through it dust by crumb. However much I rummage

I come up with nothing. I get so frantic that I finally grab the garden sieve that Tony uses to winnow the soil for his beloved pot plants and bonsais, but all to no avail. I go back inside, take the brush head off and use just the hose to vacuum along all of the little cracks between the floorboards. Still no joy. If I didn't know that they had recently had new floorboards laid, and that therefore all of the tongues were well slotted into each of their respective grooves, I would have crawled underneath the house with a torch. I check the toilet, the window ledges, the still dirty plates and even the pavement outside. Nothing.

I approach the café slowly, with a heart of base metal. I had expected Marguerite to be lunching with some friends but on opening the door I see her alone at a table by the window, toying occasionally with a salad and with a glass of red wine at her side. Her headscarf is gone and, framed as she is in a rectangle of golden sunlight, her still luxuriant silver hair glistens like a halo in some renaissance painting. Absent-mindedly, she is stroking her right earlobe. She turns to look at me and I see that dependent from her left hangs a solitary pearl, the beauty of which, dancing in the sunlight, fair takes my breath away. I cannot speak but slowly shake my head from side to side.

"Oh well," she sighs, as her shoulders gently rise and fall, "everything passes, eventually."

TOUCH

Chelsea was dead, her body floating on the surface of the Port River. There was a series of heartbreaking photographs in the *Messenger* of her mother Clementine swimming alongside, trying to coax the corpse of her two-month-old firstborn back into life by touching her, nudging her, swimming underneath and lifting her on her back so that she could breathe. She had remained by her daughter's side for three days before finally giving up the struggle and been escorted away by two more mature females. Grief was an emotion that they had all experienced. Knew that Clementine was in need of as much sympathy, companionship and physical contact as they could give her. The ever-randy males steered well clear, instead indulging their frequent impulses, as they so often did, with each other.

Grief too on the faces of the Dolphin Rangers who had gingerly paddled their inflatable alongside and gently lifted Chelsea on board so that an autopsy could be performed. It was their second recovery of a newborn calf that season.

Each year one or other of the weaker calves did not survive the legacy of pollution that humans had pumped into the estuary over many a decade. The water quality was improving with new environmental laws but a century or more of industrial outflows takes a long time to dissipate. Humans no longer swam in the waters as they once had done, and only pig-headed or desperate fishers ate their catches. Not so the dolphins of course, and although their calves would not be weaned for a couple of years, heavy metals were inevitably passed on through their mothers' milk.

Clementine would grieve for a number of weeks, but the other females in the thirty strong river pod would take turns in keeping her close, making sure that she ate sufficiently to regain her strength. Eventually she would recover from her loss and start to enjoy the touch of others again, although she probably wouldn't experience the joys of motherhood for a further couple of years.

Bob Scott folded the newspaper and cast it down on the desk of the lighthouse. He lifted his head and gazed mournfully through the open doors towards the Birkenhead Bridge, whose weed-encrusted concrete stanchions were a favourite browsing spot for any dolphin making its way upstream. Often five or six could be seen passing underneath, sometimes cruising partially surfaced to enjoy the sun on their bodies, at others taking three short breaths between shallow dives and then one much longer inhalation, before arching their backs right out of the water, giving themselves momentum for a longer, deeper dive.

Bob had never become blasé about the presence of dolphins swimming past his workplace like some of the other museum guides. During his shifts in the antique lighthouse, although he spent most of it reading novels, he was forever lifting his head to check the stretch of river visible to him. Should a glistening silver-grey back appear, or a backswept dorsal fin slice through the surface he would rush out onto the wharf to admire its passing, and to inform anyone nearby who hadn't noticed, that they were in the presence of quiet majesty. Little children became terrifically excited, their perambulating mothers grateful for the information and joyful at the expressions of wonderment on the faces of their own offspring. He had yet to come across anyone who was indifferent, although there were a few grim-faced individuals to whom he didn't impart his information, wary of a negative response. The can collector for instance, the raggedy-looking old man with his stripey bag dangling from the handlebars of his pushbike, and his straightened wire coat-hanger with which he fished in the rubbish bins. To those as obviously excited as himself he would unfurl as much of his knowledge as he judged they wanted to hear.

He tended to concentrate on descriptions of their culture: of their family relationships; their ability to communicate with one another; the herding of fish by one individual into the waiting mouths of his offsiders; the fact that they had once been land-based animals who had at some point decided to return to the seas; the fact that they had developed human sized brains something like a million years before the ancestors of homo sapiens had descended from the trees.

Some of the people that he talked to, often those wearing flowing purple robes or with lank dreadlocks and a pervasive aroma of burning vegetation, had strange ideas about the mystical aspects of their natures. They seemed to consider dolphins to have a connection to a higher, ethereal reality, as if, like Buddhist monks, they were in a constant state of meditation as they cruised their aqueous world. For this reason Bob steered clear of descriptions of their sex lives, although this was one of the areas he thought the most fascinating, one of their closest links with humans, the fact that they really enjoyed it, repeatedly. For some reason, probably an inheritance from a puritan Christian tradition, most people seemed to think that animals engage in sex only for the purposes of procreation.

Not so the dolphins. They could enjoy it three times an hour, every hour, night and day; briefly it has to be said, but repeatedly. The gender of the partner was totally unimportant, and the degree of involvement was completely up to their friend, masturbation by flipper being a perfectly acceptable substitute for penetration, and nasal sex with blow-hole perhaps being reserved for weekends or birthdays. When he read about the practice of wrapping a live wriggling eel around the penis he had wondered whether this might be regarded as a sexual perversion amongst the greater dolphin community, something akin to a leather fetish for humans, to bondage or, more appropriately, to bestiality.

No, with the general public he stuck to more acceptable observations; "Do you know that there are four countries in the world who have legislated dolphins as non-human people?" he would ask. "Isn't that brilliant? Non-human people. With rights, just like us human people."

Of course in this case it was the novelty of such language that had fascinated him. Bob Scott was a reader, always had been, always would be, and that was why this job suited him so well. It was part-time, only fifty hours a fortnight, but with penalty rates for working alternate weekends the money was sufficient for his needs. Time, that was what he treasured, for the study of serious literature what you really need is time.

His wife had a good job working as a nurse and their son was shortly to leave school. The couple had been married for nearly twenty years, the house was virtually paid off, and they led a fairly frugal, plain life. They had both been brought up in the Protestant faith, he attending the Pentecostal church in the Port and her gathering with her neighbouring Barossa Valley Lutherans. Although no longer religious they had shared the kind of formative years that seldom leave you, unless that is, you kick against the pricks. A dozen oysters each in a local pub if it had been one of his working Saturdays, a bottle of wine or two at home during the week and possibly the occasional movie, was all they felt they required.

It wasn't that they were anti-social, just self-sufficient; like their two Siamese cats they lived life unto themselves. The garden, odd improvements on the house, television or music for her in the evenings, while knitting for her numerous nephews and nieces, schoolwork on the computer for David, their son, who was hoping to do well in his Year 12 exams, and reading for Bob stretched out on the lounge or sat at the desk in his study. A quiet life. They were happy.

It hadn't always been that way. He had always been something of an outsider in the Port, uninterested as he was in sport or in drinking to excess, his school years had been a lonely endurance. He had been the butt of many a practical joke, the target of a certain amount of gratuitous bullying, from which he was only protected by his older, more athletic brother, who considered Bob to be his own personal punching bag, a sport he carried out in the privacy of their shared room at home.

"I'm only trying to toughen you up," had been his brother's excuse, but Bob knew it was simply for the pleasure of the exercise, an indulgence in the power of the strong over the weak. He endured the dead legs and the Chinese burns stoically, for attempting to fight back only invited further punishment. His one recourse, used sparingly, was to the power of words.

With language he would occasionally drive his brother away, unable to withstand a withering barrage of sarcasm. Furious, Grant would storm out of the room, lest by staying he was driven to inflicting more serious, more visible damage. Control, it was all about control, and sometimes the little shit could make him lose his totally, and that might lead to a late night appointment with the arm of a chair and their father's leather belt.

Gloriously Bob had been the first in his family and the only one of his classmates to gain, or indeed even to want, a university education. With Grant finally leaving home to get married, and channelling his aggression on behalf of the Port Adelaide Magpies, he entered into three blissful years. After graduation and then some mandatory 'overseas experience' in Europe he had become a schoolteacher. But it was the classics of literature to which he was devoted, not to shaping the minds of the disinterested country children of his first placement. So, when he had read an advertisement for a guide at the recently established Maritime Museum, he had returned thankfully to the place of his birth.

The museum had suited him perfectly. His interests also extended to history and soon he knew more than most in the institution; was able to discourse knowledgeably on any aspect of the collection, answer visitors' queries about immigration or nineteenth century navigational techniques and about the more socially acceptable aspects of the life of dolphins in the river. And on days like today, when his was just the four hour shift, he could sit in the lighthouse and read.

The work was far from onerous; taking entrance money, cleaning cases, patrolling and answering questions, doing shifts down in the lighthouse and on occasion assisting the curator change a temporary exhibition; erecting screens, hanging pictures or painting fresh colours on display panel walls. At the lighthouse there was the disbursement of bright yellow jackets to those school parties who were booked for a half-hour boat trip on the river, or attempting to instil a responsible attitude into those children who awaited their trip by climbing the winding stairs. Attempting but usually failing. In a city where most houses were single-storied, the novelty of height was too exciting, the hollow reverberation too much of an invitation to multiple screaming voices, the chance to run noisily up and down the metal latticed steps an opportunity too good to be ignored.

Having folded the newspaper away, counted the float out into the cash drawer, and hoisted the flags up to the projecting spar, Bob wound his way up the stairway to unlock and chain back the heavy metal storm-door which enabled access outside onto the viewing platform. He also ensured that the gate was secure which prevented anyone from climbing the further short flight up into the lamp-room. No one was allowed entry there for the four giant Fresnel lenses that had once revolved around the central lamp, concentrating the light into its signature flashes, floated on a bed of mercury. A metal that was liquid, to the fascination of alchemists, and which on hot days could give off undetectable yet poisonous fumes. Fumes which had driven many a lighthouse-keeper mad, as it had done the hatters of old, or at least rendered them a little strange. But then it was a job that had attracted eccentrics in the first place, men who had preferred the lonely life. Men who had wanted to forget, or perhaps to be forgotten.

Bob descended the spiral stairs, each tread a cast iron pattern of diamond holes so that you could see down through them, causing many a visitor a vertiginous descent, which when combined with the claustrophobia of the confined metal tube they were encased in, and the repeated nautilus turns, left them shaking when they finally returned to terra firma. Bob himself was not unaffected by heights and had forced himself up on his very first shift, repeating in his head, "I need the job, I need the job." He had climbed the ten narrower steps of the steep and straight final flight up to the platform level on his hands and knees, forcing himself not to look down into the dark throat that gaped beneath him. Nowadays, of course, with the familiarity of years, he had no such problems, although when it was time to shut he was reluctant to walk around outside on the platform, preferring to shout "anyone still up here?" before unchaining and locking the door closed. He would occasionally wake, sweating in the backwash of a nightmare, with the sickening feeling that he had left someone with a hearing impairment locked out up there overnight.

One more task remained to be performed, wheeling out the PFDs on their wheeled racks, ready for the visiting group scheduled for a trip on the motor launch *Archie Badenoch*. Life jackets they had used to call them, but not anymore. "It might worry the children unnecessarily," they had been told by management. Apparently Personal Flotation Devices had no such threatening implications.

It was school holidays so today it would be an Out of School Hours Care party, the kind of group the guides disliked dealing with the most. Such wide mixtures of various ages were often loud and unruly, not disciplined by their teachers like a term-time visiting class. Frequently they would be shepherded by volunteer mums or by youth workers and trainee teachers not much older than their charges, earning a few bucks in their vacations, with no real authority and less hope of control. Half the group would ascend the lighthouse stairs, often shouting and screaming as they went, and sometimes spitting down from above, while the other half were taken out on the river, hopefully to catch sight of some dolphins, before the two groups swapped over. Luckily, according to the roster, today's was to be a small party, just twenty children with two carers who could all embark on the *Archie* at once, and then do the lighthouse climb all together afterwards.

Having wheeled out the jackets, Bob returned to his desk and the glories of Spenser's *Faerie Queen*. He was reading the lines gently under his breath, when a woman poked her head in through the door and he realised that the group had arrived. She was tall, about six feet Bob reckoned, with a dark complexion and such a head of waving crow-black hair that Bob wondered if she had Spanish ancestry. He could imagine her clicking casta-nets and imperiously stamping her long legs to the tune of a gypsy guitar, a picture that was soon dissipated when she opened her mouth and with a nasal wine informed him that "We're here for the boat trip," with that rising inflection which appears to turn all statements into questions.

"Sure. I'll come out. All of the children have to be kitted out in one of those life...I mean PFDs. There are two sizes. Here, let me show you."

So Bob was outside, being mobbed by children as he tried to hand them out to the carer and her shorter, plumper offsider. Both of the women were in their late thirties he estimated, his flamenco dancer obviously in charge, the other nervously biting on her lower lip. He explained that the double-strapped ones were bigger, and that the zips had to be done up before the straps were fastened across with the plastic clips. Then he tried to leave them to it although the boys, of course, were grabbing them out of his hands in their eagerness, and once suited up started bouncing off each other's chests or pretending to be junior Sumo wrestlers. The girls, just as eager but somehow more polite, reached them out of his hands and followed his instructions. Once they were all equipped Bob was about to return to his desk when he noticed one young girl who was crying in frustration at her inability to strap herself in.

She was a beautiful little thing, possibly five or six years old, wearing a blue tee-shirt and pink leggings, her shoulder length hair so soft and so blonde that it was almost white, and her eyes and cheeks flaming red from crying. She had managed to get the zip done up all the way but did not have enough strength in her tiny fingers to manipulate the plastic catches that fastened the belt across the front. She looked worried that the others might go without her, was terrified of being left behind.

The two female carers hadn't noticed the little girl weeping as they were too busy trying to get a jacket onto a confused and recalcitrant older Down's Syndrome girl, who seemed determined to put it on back to front.

Bob was torn. He so longed to reach out to the little girl and do up the clip, he couldn't stand to watch the beautiful little creature in her agony when all he had to do was to kneel down and fasten it for her. But he wasn't allowed. Strict instructions had come down from above that under no circumstances were any of the guides to touch any child in any way whatsoever. Such was the current paranoia about paedophilia that absolutely no contact was permitted, no matter that all of the guides and the volunteers who crewed the old launch had undergone police checks, no matter that all of them were parents themselves, grandparents too, some of them. There was the new rule and it had to be strictly adhered to, a rule that had again been emphasised in the previous week's staff meeting. So, helpless, and feeling like the coldest-hearted bastard that he could imagine, Bob turned away from the agonized child and retreated into the lighthouse. Thankfully one of the older girls finally noticed the little one's tears and, after throwing a disgusted look in his direction, bent down and did what was required, afterwards giving her a comforting hug. Bob sighed with relief as the whole party moved off towards the pontoon where the *Archie* was moored and he could return to the poetic delights of an earlier, more chivalric age.

Half an hour later they returned and one by one handed him their life preservers, whilst they told him exaggerated stories of the number of dolphins they had seen. One young lad informed him that they had seen hundreds, whilst another recounted how many jellyfish had been in the river. He smiled and agreed with everything he was told. They were all terribly excited by the prospect of climbing the lighthouse, with the older ones pressing forwards, impatient to get started. He tried to calm them down by explaining the rules about no running, staying in single file and not pushing in on the stairs, warnings that he knew would likely be completely disregarded once they were out of his sight, so reinforced them by stating that one of the carers should go first, with the other bringing up the rear in case someone decided half way that they didn't like heights.

"Are you not coming with us?" the tall woman asked, surprised and seemingly disappointed not to have an official take control over her charges.

"No, I have to stay down here to take money from anyone else who wants to climb," he responded. "They are totally your responsibility, I'm afraid."

It amazed him how often he had had to say this over the years. His job was just to keep the facility open so that groups like hers could enjoy them, as well as other museum visitors and the occasional passing tourist.

As he returned to his desk she threw him a haughty look, as if she considered that he was failing in his responsibilities, no doubt having been contemplating the prospect of sitting down on the bench outside with a coffee whilst he took over. She led her crocodile towards the staircase. The children were laughing and some of them asked him how many steps there were, as they slowly passed his little office.

"Well, how about you count them, then I'll tell you if you're right when you get back down."

"That's a good idea," the woman who waited at the rear told him with a wry smile, as if apologising for her brusque fellow carer. "Come on children, let's all count them."

A mother, he thought, not a professional. Thankfully he returned to his book.

Twenty minutes later he was wrenched out of his pleasant reverie by a piercing scream from above. Then another, and again another.

"What the hell?" He leaped from his chair and ran to stand at the foot of the stairs. Looking up he could not see what the problem was as the repeated turns of the staircase obstructed a clear view. The screaming continued intermittently but now he could also hear an adult voice shouting commands.

"Pull yourself together, Leslie. You can't just sit there."

He could also hear footsteps clattering down and suddenly five children appeared around the last turn. Three of them were laughing as they came.

"What's going on?"

"Oh, it's just Leslie. She's frightened," the boy who had seen jellyfish said, with a smirk on his face.

"Is she hurt?"

"No," a little girl said, "she's just a bit strange."

"She shouldn't have come, she always spoils things," from another small boy.

"Stand up, Leslie, there's nothing to be frightened of." This from above, followed by another burst of screams and then, "Oh, be quiet, you're just working yourself up."

"You five better stay in here," Bob indicated his office. "Don't go running off. I'll go up and see." He didn't like to leave them alone, the edge of the wharf was only a few metres away and they were clearly over-excited. He turned and started to run up the stairs, the noise from above growing louder as he climbed.

As he turned the last gyre of the spiral he found himself staring into the tortured face of the little girl with Down's, who was lying on the floor of the metal platform with the dark-haired carer towering over her, obviously having lost her temper. She was shouting at the poor waif, trying to overtop her screams and ordering her to be sensible. Meanwhile crowded onto the straight ladder section behind them were the rest of the children, held back by the other carer. This more maternal woman, whilst obviously not feeling able to interfere with the group leader, was trying to damp down their agitated comments which clearly were not helping the situation.

Bob couldn't believe it. How the tall, domineering woman could think that just by standing over her and shouting, she could persuade the tiny little confused and obviously terrified mite at her feet to uncurl from her foetal position, stand up and walk into what she perceived akin to the jaws of death.

"She just *won't* move," the exasperated woman told him.

"Yes, I can see that. Meanwhile there are five children down there with nobody looking after them. Perhaps if you could let the others squeeze past, it would calm things down a bit."

"Good idea," from the woman on the steps, and so saying she began to shepherd the rest of the flock past the two protagonists, locked into their conflicted positions. When they had gingerly picked their way around the frozen tableau Bob moved as far as he could to one side, onto the narrowest portion of the wedged-shaped step, so that one by one they could edge past him.

"Now, Leslie isn't it?" Standing as he was several steps below the platform his head was on the same level as the little girl's as she lay curled up on the floor. "See, there they go Leslie, they are all Ok, aren't they? There's really nothing to be frightened of." This provoked another wail from the small child, but at least it wasn't quite at the same piercing level as her previous screams.

"This is my lighthouse Leslie, and I have been up and down here hundreds of times. It really is very safe." More wails, but Bob could see that he was getting through to her somehow, she was paying attention to him, looking into his face, as if the furious statuesque figure looming behind her had been totally obliterated from her consciousness. Luckily she didn't appear to even hear her as she pitched in with "You have to go down, you just can't stay up here all day." Bob nearly shot the virago a withering look in an effort to shut her up, but rather kept his eyes focussed on the vulnerable little one, looking straight into her frightened eyes.

"How about if you held my hand Leslie, then we could walk down together," as he held out his hand. She flinched away from it a little and another wail wrenched from her fragile little body. This was obviously not a possibility.

"Ok Leslie, Ok, no one's going to force you," as he slowly withdrew his hand. He was pretty much out of options now until a sudden thought occurred to him. Bob hadn't had any personal experience of children with Down's Syndrome, but he was aware of the general consensus that they were usually particularly happy and loving individuals. He had heard older parents on afternoon radio programs worrying about what was to happen to their offspring when they were no longer able to care for them, because of their very trusting natures, of how naturally affectionate they were. He figured that Leslie was probably used to a lot of physical contact from her parents, a lot of cuddles, a lot of touching, and that this small lost child was probably used to being picked up a lot by her father and mother.

"How about if I carried you down, Leslie, would you like that?" The crying stopped instantly and looking deep into his eyes she slowly nodded her head.

"Alright, come here then little one," and he stepped up and scooped her into his arms.

He was worried, of course. He hadn't carried his own child in his arms for ten years, when he had been a younger, much stronger man. She was not that light. Moreover, whenever he negotiated these seventy winding stairs on his own he usually kept one steadying hand on the hand-rail. Still, they slowly descended, one step at a time, with her arms flung around his neck, her eyes closed and her head pressed firmly into his shoulder, his arms crossed under to support her bottom and her outflung legs gripping his waist tightly. All he thought about was maintaining his balance, treading as gently as possible so that she wouldn't suddenly be jolted back into terror, causing her to jerk and possibly toppling the pair of them.

Finally they reached the ground and he gently placed the little girl's feet back on the ground. The other children were waiting to see what would happen and had been standing around the door of the lighthouse where the mother of one of them had them gathered. As soon as they saw the pair of them regain the ground they all broke into a burst of frenzied clapping. Leslie ran towards them, happily smiling, her ordeal seemingly completely wiped from her memory. Bob, embarrassed by the applause from a motley collection of six- to twelve-year-olds, his face blushing a livid red, smiled and waved and retired quickly into his little office.

Later, when Bill came to relieve him from his shift, he explained how his morning had gone.

"Good on you. But you know what you've got to do now, don't you?"

"What?"

"Go back to the office, and explain how and why you've touched a child. Just in case someone makes a complaint."

"She wouldn't dare."

"She might, if you made her feel inadequate."

"Jesus bloody Christ."

THERE'S A DARKNESS

A confusion of sounds. Ticking, pinging noises, murmuring voices, incomprehensible, maybe foreign, although why would they be? Where the hell was he? Weird smell, sort of rubbery, or...no, nothing he could recognise. Sliding sounds, something vaguely wheeled occasionally passing by, a large acoustic, a sensation of space, but hollow, not like he was lying in the open air even though ants are crawling around on him, itching. Trying to scratch, brush them off but he can't move. Why can't he move? And why the hell can't he see anything? Panic. Panic! Heart-wrench, gut-wrench; fear. He's tied down, he can't move, and ants are crawling on him, particularly around his crotch. Stretched out across an ant-hill like a victim in a boyhood comic? People he can't understand are hovering around the place and he can't bloody see. As much as he tries he just can't force his eyelids up.

Then someone close-by groans. And someone on his other side, further away, whimpers, as if conversing across his body in a language of pain.

A conversation he is excluded from for he cannot open his mouth either, is utterly helpless, locked up tight within a bone walled prison where he can only receive, can in no way participate. What are they going to do to him? What have they done already? And who the hell are they? Then, on the back of his eyelids, an angel with soft brushed wings and a vaguely familiar face opened wide her arms and into them he gratefully fell.

Later, coming back up, it seemed as if someone suddenly ripped off the tape that had locked shut his eyes, like gaffer tape ripped from the mouth of a hostage.

Bed. He was in a bed, not tied across an anthill as he had feared. His legs were hidden beneath some kind of arched structure covered by a flannelette sheet. That is if he still had legs. There was pain, but that meant nothing; he had watched enough television in his relatively short life to be aware of phantom feelings in absent limbs. He had to see, no matter the effort involved in moving a bandaged arm, no matter the cascade of sweat erupting above his eyebrows. Gradually he was able to lift the edge of the sheet with the back of a stiffly bandaged hand. They were both there!

Overwhelmed with relief his arm dropped to the mattress again, although he flinched at the vision he had been afforded of the metal pins that pierced his skin on either side of the one on the left. Steel and flesh were to him an alien, unholy marriage of elements. A sight to which he was psychically allergic. When he was little, Wendy had taken him with her to visit one of her friends who had fallen off the back of a motorbike and had her jaw rewired. He had thrown up right there on the hospital floor.

"You're awake," a voice said from somewhere off to his side and a figure in a green tunic and matching pants emerged into his field of view and wrote something on a clipboard.

"Where...?" His throat rasped.

"In hospital. Intensive care. You've had an accident." As she said this she did something to a valve on a plastic bag which was suspended from a chrome armature by his side. A clear plastic tube ran down to burrow beneath the bandages tightly encasing his left arm.

"Where's Tom?"

"Rest. Sleep," and she jotted something else on her clipboard, before hanging it over the end of the bed. She poured water from a jug beside him into a baby's feeding cup and held it to his mouth, encouraging him to drink. He wondered why she had avoided lifting his head. Placing the empty cup back onto his bedside table she smiled and withdrew through a door he had not noticed before. After a few moments, or maybe an hour later, the door reopened and a Salvation Army silver band marched in, played "Onward Christian Soldiers" with gusto as they three times circled around his bed, before disappearing the way they had come in. "If you're looking for the angel you've just missed her," he tried to say as he slipped back under where he found her waiting for him. At first he was pleased to see her.

The angel spread wide her wings and rushed headlong towards him, but as she flew she changed. Her wings turned into branches, feathers morphed into leaves, and she heaved her roots up, massive roots with arthritic knuckles, fingers dripping soil as they relinquished their earthly grip and reached out for him, clutching at his arms and legs in a dark and painful embrace.

He woke up screaming.

"It's alright, you're safe now. Shush, shush. You're going to be just fine."

The voice was back. He turned his head. The woman in the green scrubs was by his side again.

"What's happening?"

"I told you yesterday. You're in hospital. You've had an accident. You were in a car crash. And now you're in intensive care."

"My legs…"

"Are broken, but they'll mend, are mending. How do you feel?"

He thought about that. "Can't move. And the ants…"

"There are no ants."

"Crawling all over me. Itchy. Can't move my hands. Can't scratch. They're driving me crazy."

"It's probably the morphine. Some people are allergic to it. I'll get them to change your pain relief."

Normality was returning and he didn't want it, so he closed his eyes and fell back to sleep.

When he awoke he was in a different room and his mother sat by his bedside. She looked a little like the angel who had visited his dreams, but her face more haggard, lined with worry. She was wearing a dress, which was unusual, and she was chewing on one of her strands of hair.

"Hello," she said as she pulled it from her mouth.

"What happened to me?"

"Don't you remember?"

"Not much. I was in a car. With Tom. Where's Tom?"

About ten o'clock there's a ring on the bell so I open the door and there's Tom. "Hi stranger," I say, tentative like, 'cos I haven't seen him for over a year and I'm wondering if he's come round to punch me out for what I did in his mother's undies. But he just jangles a bunch of car keys in my face and says "Fancy coming for a ride?"

"Shit yeh," I reply and I scribble a note for Wendy on the kitchen table 'cos it's a Friday night and she's out at the club with her mate Mary. It's their night for going dancing. 'Grab a Granny' I call it which is a bit unfair 'cos they've both only just turned forty but the filthy looks they throw my way split me. Besides Mary's daughter had a baby last year, so.

Then we're out on the street and I'm looking at the wheels. A Jag! Fuck! "That ain't yours," I say. I mean fair enough it's pretty old, a Mark Two, early sixties I reckon, but it's in beaut condition. I know a bit about cars, I used to collect Matchbox. I've never actually been inside a Jag.

"Nah, one of the old man's toys. I live at his place these days. He and the Bimbo flew up to Port Augusta yesterday on a case so I've borrowed it for the weekend."

"When d'you get your license?"

"Don't need one, do I."

"How's that?"

"My dad's a lawyer," and he cracks up laughing. "Come on, get in."

I've been walking all around the metallic silver feline, almost reaching out to stroke it, and sticking a finger between the jaws of the pouncing jaguar on the front. The flying girl on a Roller is pretty cool, but for absolutely awesome nothing beats the predatory chrome creatures leaping off the bonnets of these mechanical beasts. "You want speed?" they seem to demand, "I'll give you speed. All taut sinew and lithe muscle, full torque and energy, and elemental downright Growl!"

"Hurry up," Tom says and I slide onto a seat of red leather luxury, inhaling the warm scent of tanned flesh and closing the door with a satisfyingly solid clunk, like the sound of a bank vault closing, or the dead sound of a shutting prison door.

"Nice eh? Dad spent a fortune restoring it. Nought to sixty in ten seconds he reckons. Top speed nearly 200 klicks. He took me on a run once. Unbelievable."

"So where we going?"

"I got a bit of business to transact down here then we'll take her for a bit of a burn, Ok?"

"Let's go!"

"What the hell did the two of you think you were doing?" Jack had never seen his mother so angry although he could tell by the taut look on her face she was trying to control it. Trying to be sympathetic. What the hell had he been doing? Just gone out for a drive was what he'd thought.

We turn left at the cement works and cruise down Victoria Road past the petrol stations by the old Hardie's asbestos factory and the giant cylinders of the Caltex storage tanks, turn right into an abandoned industrial area and pull up by a three metre high corrugated iron fence that, surprisingly, is unadorned by graffiti like most of the other structures littering the side road. We get out and Tom raps on a section of fence that looks like it could be a gate. I notice two security cameras peering down at us from either side.

"You ever been here before?" he asks.

"Nah."

"Best club in town," and he laughs. "Exclusive though. You'll be right, you're with me. Have a couple of beers while I go see the man. It won't take long."

A small section of tin slides back and a dark hairy face with three crude blue stars tattooed under the left eye appears.

"Yeh, what d'you want?"

"I've got an appointment with Manny."

"Tom are yuh? Who's he?"

"That's Jack. He's my mate, he's alright."

"You'd better come in then."

"Tom was speeding. He lost control and drove into one of those Moreton Bay fig trees, hit one of those bloody great roots they have. The car rolled and you were flung out. The coppers said you flew."

"What coppers?"

"The ones who found you. The ones who were chasing you."

The gate swings back with a rasp of unoiled metal and we walk across the compound towards an old breeze-block factory building, passing through two neat rows of motor bikes, all with their front wheels turned sideways back towards the gate, military formation style, ready for instant action. Big bikes, all black and highly polished chrome, Harleys most of them but I notice the odd old BSA amongst them and one dark behemoth with Indian inscribed on its petrol tank. There are more cameras covering the bikes.

As we near the building I hear the sound of AC/DC leaking out around the doorframe; there are no windows. Back in Black. Something of an anthem. The gatekeeper opens the door and the sound pounds me straight in the chest, the bass vibrating my lungs. He ushers us inside with an oily thumb before returning to his post out front.

The place is heaving. There are thirty or so people I can make out through the haze of tobacco and, possibly, other smoke. Mostly men in leather jackets, although a few girls in short denim skirts are dancing together over by the massive speakers whilst a bunch of hungry looking guys survey their gyrations. Another couple of leggy molls are draped over the thighs of two big men sunk into one of the broken-hearted lounges that are scattered throughout. The hulks are deep in converse with each other, seemingly unaware of the women perched upon them. At one end of the room a couple of bearded and long-haired giants are taking turns on a full-sized pool table, intermittently chugging down on jugs of beer. Through the throng I make out that the long wall facing us is almost completely covered by two enormous flags, both adorned by stars, one with the Southern Cross of Australia and the other bearing the cross of the Confederate States of America, now become the universal symbol of outlaws. Between the two hangs down a piece of black cloth, emblazoned upon it in gold and red I recognise what they call a caduceus; a winged-headed staff entwined by two serpents. It's an emblem familiar to residents of the Port, usually seen on a disappearing back as it roars off, thankfully, down a road.

"Oh God," I think to myself, "we're in the Snakebites' fortress. What the hell are we doing here?"

I don't have time to ask as Tom grips my arm and steers me towards the bar that spans the far wall.

"What'll it be boys?" asks the black-singleted barman with the full Ned Kelly sprouting from his jaw. "You ain't members so you get full price but we got pretty much anything you'd care to imbibe. 'Cepting milk that is," and he laughs, revealing a row of jagged and discoloured teeth.

"Coupla beers," says Tom, "Coopers Pale thanks. Manny about?"

"I'll get him for you," and he presses a button with one hand as he pulls the beers with the other.

A door opens to one side of the rows of optics and a small guy with a ratty face and thick tinted glasses appears, nods to Tom, then raises a flap and invites him through.

"I got to talk to this guy for a minute. Just stay here, enjoy your beer," Tom tells me.

Jesus, I feel abandoned, lost like a kitten in a bear-pit. I stare into my beer until a hand slaps me on the back. I jump and nearly spill beer down my shirt but when I turn I see a face I recognise, one I haven't seen since school.

"Lippy, Christ you made me jump, how are you?" We have to shout at each other. Early Stones are now rocking the joint. Sympathy for the Devil.

"No one calls me that no more. I'm Sundance. Sunny for short." So saying he stroked his drooping moustache.

At school he used to have a scar on his upper lip from corrective surgery, now he sports a blond Robert Redford style Zapata.

"What're you doing here, Jack?"

"Fucked if I know. Tom brought me. You remember Tom? He went off through there."

"Ah."

"What about you? You a Snakebite now?"

"Just a prospect. Shouldn't be a problem though, my old man's the Sergeant-at-Arms. That's him on the pool table," he nods towards one of the giants lining up a shot.

"It's not what you know..."

"It's who," he completes. "Way of the world, man, way of the fucking world. Just ask Tom. Tell you what though, you

98

weren't one of the worst creeps at that shithole. Take care of yourself," and he drifts off back to his mates as he sees Tom re-emerging from behind the bar with rat-face, who walks outside.

"We leaving now?" I ask.

"Soon. Manny's just gone to get me something. He'll text me, then we can split. Was that Lippy?"

"He's Sunny now, yeh."

"We never hit it off."

"No."

"C'mon, drink up, it won't be long."

"They were chasing you through the parklands. High speed. Tom lost control."

"Is he in here too?"

"Not anymore. The cops said he was on drugs. They found stuff in the car. You were clean though, they tested your blood. I guess there was lots of it. They'll be wanting to talk to you. Don't you remember anything?"

"Bits and pieces I suppose. I think I remember the tree."

"The nurses said it'll probably come back to you. But don't say anything to them. You weren't driving and you weren't stoned, thank God. Just stick to that and they won't be able to twist anything. What the hell were the two of you doing?"

"Tom was getting something."

"The drugs?"

"Well, yeh."

Outside there's no sign of Manny but Tom reaches down and extracts a package from behind one of the rear wheels. We get in and he chucks it onto the rear seat.

"Just got to check out the merchandise. Let's go up to Largs."

So we're in the car park just below the old fort. Behind us you can just make out the barrels of the two massive cannons that were supposed to keep the Russian fleet from entering the Port River, sometime back in the nineteenth century. Tom and I had sneaked into the fort one night after history class, playing at firing the obsolete cannons at phantom ships attempting their covert invasion, until we were chased out by one of the officers from the Police Academy whose now abandoned regimented buildings still occupy the site next door.

Now we're back, parked up and looking down over the wavering shadows of the scrub covered sandhills and beyond, to the silver streak of moonlight like an illuminated pathway over darkling waters, inviting memory's embrace.

Tom reaches for and opens the package, pulls a little glass pipe out of the glovebox into which he sprinkles a white powder, fires it up with a Bic lighter on high and takes a big drag.

"Oh yeh," he says as he exhales contentedly, "that does the fucking trick."

"What is it?" I ask after a few minutes, although I've already twigged.

"The real deal, is what it is. Skank, Glass, Crystal Meth. You watch Breaking Bad?"

"Coupla times. Couldn't stand the sight of that old guy wandering about in those disgusting old Y-fronts."

"Your loss, it's a great show."

"Yeh, maybe. So you an addict now?"

Tom looks annoyed. "Nah. Just like a toke now and again. This lot ain't for me, it's for a couple of the guys. They reckon it helps with their work. Advertising's a pretty full-on business. I told them I got contacts and they let me have a gram or two for getting it. You want a hit?"

So here I am. Moment of choice. I've smoked plenty of weed at one time or another, like most of the kids at the old school. You grow up in the Port you can't really avoid it. Half the parents grow some in their back yards. It's Ok at parties, makes you feel pretty good. Makes me bloody horny too, but kind of self-conscious at the same time, so I don't get to do much about it, not until I get home that is. This is different, though. This is grown-up drugs. Serious shit.

I don't want Tom to think I'm scared, but the truth is, I am. I mean what am I? What have I got? Bugger all. I'm eighteen, I live with, and off, my mother who has to clean other people's houses to support us. I have a shitty little schoolboy's job delivering papers for pocket money. No prospects of anything better 'cos there's no work around here. No wheels apart from a crappy old bike that's too small for me. No smart clothes to wear even if I did get an interview somewhere. No hope, no future. No real mates even, not since I sussed that Tom only came round 'cos he didn't want to walk into the Snakebite fortress on his own. Either that or he wanted to show off what a big man he's become. Probably both. Not even a gang like Lippy. Be different if I could play guitar or sing or something, then I could start up a band like some of them did, play around some of the pubs. But I got no real talent for anything. And now Tom has refilled his pipe and is offering me a toke on something that might take all of this away. Get me hooked on something that would mean I didn't have to care anymore.

"Go on, try it man, the rush is fucking beautiful."

"No thanks," I say, "can't afford to get addicted."

"One little toke won't hurt you."

"No," again, more forcefully.

"What's the bloody problem? You always liked a bit of weed." Seems like he's getting angry now.

"That's different. Organic ain't it. Grows in the bloody ground. You know what you're getting. Not this chemical shit. You got no idea. They reckon they use rat poison and all sorts."

"That's just bullshit to scare people. You see me frothing at the mouth?"

"Course not."

"Well then, take a fucking hit," and he tries to put the pipe into my hand.

Maybe he's right. Maybe it is all just propaganda. That's not really what scares me though. It's me. I believe the stuff about addiction. And I know I'm vulnerable. It would be so easy to just slip into the darkness. And then what? A life of crime trying to feed the habit? Gaol? A wasted life?

I've seen plenty of old no-hopers just hanging around doing bugger all, propping up bars on dole-day, hoping to score some weed. They're bad enough. Worse are the match-stick people queuing up outside the chemist's on Commercial Road to get their methadone scripts filled. And there's plenty of damaged souls shacked up in halfway houses round here. Ok, they're mostly alkies, but some of them are probably drug-fucked acid casualties. I know I can't say it to Tom, but there's no way I could do that to Wendy. The shame she would feel. She'd probably blame herself. Ok, if that makes me a 'Mummy's-boy' so be it but I'm buggered if I'm going to let Tom accuse me of it. So I come on a bit strong.

"Look, I just don't want to, alright? Sure, I like a bit of weed now and again, but I didn't want to go to no bikie fortress, and I sure as hell don't want to smoke any of that shit they peddle."

"Ok, Ok, keep your fucking hair on."

"I thought we was just going for a ride in a classic car. Not some frigging drug run."

"Your loss," he says, "I was just trying to do you a favour. You don't know what you're missing."

"I'm cool with that."

"Oh well, 'waste not want not'. I'll just have to smoke it," he says, waving the pipe in my face. "Then we'll go for that ride I promised you. Hey, I'll take you back to Dad's place, show you how I'm living now, it's way cool."

"You safe to drive on that?"

"Sure, once I'm over the initial rush, won't be long," and he fires up again.

I open the window to get rid of the stink and sit there enjoying the view of moonlight on dark waters and the sound of waves sloughing over shifting sands. After ten minutes or so he turns the key in the ignition.

"Hear that purr," he says. "The beast awakens."

"You sure you're Ok?"

"It's speed, man. It speeds up your reactions. Why the Japs and the Germans used it in the war. Be the safest drive you've ever had."

He sprays gravel as we reverse around in the car park and roar off towards town.

"The little bastard!"

"Come on Mum, he's my mate."

"Was your mate."

"What?"

"Haven't they told you? You were flung out of the car when it rolled. Appears you weren't wearing a seat belt. Tom wasn't so lucky."

"Oh shit."

"I don't care. He nearly killed you too. I'm sorry but I'm bloody angry. With both of you."

"He was off his face."

"Shouldn't have got in the car then, should you?"

"He said he could handle it."

"Oh yeh, he handled it alright, straight into a bloody tree."

"Mum!"

"Sorry love. I'd better go. This can't be helping. It's just the shock, or maybe the relief, I don't know. I'll be better tomorrow, now you've woken up. I lost your dad and now I've nearly lost you, I couldn't stand that again."

"Sorry Mum."

"It's not your fault. It's that bloody, stuck up…"

"He was my mate."

"Yeh, well. Look, I'll be back in tomorrow. And I promise to be in a better mood. You just lie there, do what the nurses tell you and get better. I want you home with me. And remember what I said about the cops. It was all Tom's fault, so don't get involved. I've already had his mother round, saying you must have been to blame. And God knows how his father will try to twist it."

She pulled her hair back from her face, and as she leant across to kiss him Tom caught a slight whiff of alcohol on her breath. He regretted causing her pain; the stiffener she had felt

104

she needed to come in to see him. He was relieved when she left. He was tired, but needed time to process the information. Tom was dead.

Tom drives back down the peninsula, across the hump of the Birkenhead Bridge so fast I think we're going to take off, slows down for the sets of lights through the Port, then he cranks it up for the long straight of the Port Road back into Adelaide. It must be somewhere along here the cops see us flash past and start to follow. After a while I hear their siren wailing, turn my head and see their flashing lights.

"Shit!" says Tom and instead of slowing down and pulling over he floors it, tells me to hang on, and veers off up a side road with a scream of tyres. He's laughing, the stupid bastard; I look and there's a mask-like grin on his face; he's enjoying himself, like he's playing some game; like the windscreen and the mirrors have all turned into video screens, and he's at the controls, he's manipulating reality. He tears around corners, jinks about in the side streets, narrowly misses parked cars, bounces over speed bumps, flies straight across at intersections.

"Slow down!" I scream at some point, "you'll get us both killed!" But he doesn't listen, just laughs again and says, "Don't be such a chicken. We'll beat them easy. Anyway, we can't get caught with that stuff in the car."

We lurch from side to side and I've lost all track of where we are until I see from the trees that we've hit the Parklands, but the cop lights are still flashing behind us and soon we'll be amongst the traffic in town.

Tom must have realised that he can't escape them 'cos he shouts to me to "get rid of the gear!" It's this that saves me 'cos I undo my seat belt to turn to get the package off the back seat *just as he screams "Road spikes! Shit!" and he swerves wildly and there's this huge God Almighty BANG! and I'm wrenched out through the window.*

"You flew," says the cop who's sitting by my bedside when I wake up again. "Spectacular it was. I thought you were a goner for sure. You were lucky we were so close to the hospital, the ambos were there pretty bloody quick." He seemed like a nice guy, probably only a few years older than me. I reckon he had enjoyed the chase, felt bad about Tom and was genuinely glad that I had survived.

He wasn't alone. There was a plain clothes with him. "Couple of broken legs, nasty crack on the skull, and scraped the skin off your arms. Coulda been a lot worse. Like your mate."

The uniform got up to leave. "Just came to see how you were. I'll leave you to it," as he nodded to the other one. Who was there to grill me about the drugs. Whose were they? Where had we got them? Where were we going with them? All that.

I couldn't remember a thing. Severe bang to my head. Wiped all of it from my memory. Only that they weren't mine. Never touched the filthy stuff. Must have been Tom's. Or maybe his dad's, it was his car after all. That got him interested, pounced on it like a dog at a Christmas dinner, or a cop nipping at the heels of a lawyer, but I couldn't say for sure, I had absolutely no idea. I held on firmly to what Wendy had said. It was lucky that the crash had happened just as I was reaching for it, so it had no fingerprints from me. He grilled me, and grilled me, but I just couldn't remember. So, in the end, grumpy, he pissed off. Leaving me to mourn for my mate who, for whatever reason, had slipped, head first, straight out into the darkness.

ANGEL

Angel was an education. She told me many things. Of how it was to live as a single Western woman in Japan, and how proudly her Japanese lover would show her off to his friends, as if she were some kind of talisman. Of how she had luxuriated, for a while, in the cloak of exoticism that he had draped around her.

She told me of a museum he had taken her to, where the exhibits were the skins flayed from peoples' backs; framed, displayed and delicately lit because of the exquisite tattoos that had adorned their bodies when alive. She revelled in the thought that the owners of these walking canvasses could only glimpse their priceless masterpieces reversed in occasional mirrors, or possibly in specially constructed private opticons, where they might give themselves up to their solitary pleasures.

She spoke of wolf-howling, freezing nights slowly rattling across a continent in the Trans-Siberian Express, travelling back towards the place she no longer thought of as home, smuggling in her bejewelled portmanteau the cloak that was to adorn her consciousness from that time on.

She told me stories as she smoked her French cigarettes and confessed that she was trying to cut down to only one an hour. She didn't succeed, and finally paid the price. She was the most intellectual and sophisticated woman that I had ever met. The first true feminist I encountered; a real-life bohemian; a femme fatale straight out of Hollywood casting, ten years my senior, one hundred years more experienced. She taught me how to properly make love to a woman, a lesson that they had signally failed to impart at my all male school, which had led to my presumably unsatisfied wife having run off with someone I had once considered a friend.

When she found out that I was desirous of becoming a writer she told me that I should stop smoking dope because it saps the will-power; that I should travel because it expands the horizons; but that firstly I should go to university because it increases the self-confidence. When I finally did, some twenty years later and in a country ten thousand miles away, it was to find that she was one of the authors I was to study.

When we met I was living in a small village six miles south of Bath, catching the train in every morning, and walking through town to the furniture shop of which I was nominally the manager, situated at the bottom of steep Lansdown Hill. I say nominally because I was the sole employee. The shop specialised in furniture made of cane imported from the Far East, or else constructed out of willow withies, some from the nearby Somerset Levels, but mostly from the floundering economies of Eastern Europe. My little enterprise was the offshoot of a larger household design emporium, one of many that had sprung up to exploit the growing affluence of the colour-supplemented sixties.

It was situated at the point of the triangle where Lansdown Road meets the elegant curve of the once-grand but later soot-blackened Paragon, before both sweep round into George Street. The shop was afforded angled windows on both sides and one large one which truncated the point and stared magisterially over the junction down into Broad Street, a name redolent of the looms which had once provided the wealth of the city. That was before a collection of Georgian gentlemen architects transformed it into the first domestic tourist destination. No longer were the leisured classes forced to undertake foreign travel, with its difficulties of language and inadequate sewage arrangements. They could stay in this Venice of the North, gain or lose fortunes at the turn of a card, bathe in and take the waters, dress-up, attend concerts, flirt, conduct illicit relationships, and generally show themselves off.

Limited as it was in the type of goods purveyed, my shop was quiet for long periods every day. People wanting unusual garden furniture for the patios, conservatories and gazebos which graced the elegant manors, farms or converted millhouses scattered throughout the surrounding countryside were the usual clientele. Professionals on their way up, wives of commuting businessmen, university lecturers, all manner of the well-off bourgeoisie who over the last decade had re-discovered the delights of Georgian architecture. The revolution of oil-fired central heating had rendered liveable again the high ceilinged rooms which had been so shunned in the freezing forties and fifties, servants being 'so hard to find' in the aftermath of war. I remember one middle-aged and tweed-jacketed customer who, on seeing my quizzical look at the signature on his cheque, drawn on a bank of which I had never heard, had explained that he was, in fact, the Duke of that particular county. Luckily for me he was, and not some wandering con artist, whatever his ancestors might have been.

There were also the merely curious; people who wanted to know, just once, what it felt like to occupy an ornate peacock throne, or recline upon a woven chaise-longue, imagining boys providing gin-slings on the veranda of some Malayan rubber plantation. With some of these casual visitors I had many an interesting conversation. The elderly woman who with her deceased husband had been enthusiastic Party members until the Soviet invasion of Hungary, or the one-eyed gentleman who had lost the other at the siege of Tobruk, who informed me that he had much more success with the ladies when wearing his rakish eyepatch, than he did with his glass eye naked. "It disturbs them," he said, "when one eye moves and the other one don't." He had come into the shop because the chairs in the window had reminded him of a particular bordello that he and his mates had joyfully frequented in Cairo. Initially I had thought that Angel would be another one of these.

It was quiet, as usual, and as usual I was reading a book. Apart from taking any deliveries, sweeping the varnished floorboards, and replacing an occasional piece from the basement there was very little else for me to do. Now and again my boss would walk up from his more extensive store in Broad Street and I would suddenly have to look busy rearranging the window displays, but generally most of my time was spent ensconced in a book. It wasn't well paid but it was an excellent job for a bibliophile like myself. And since the furniture was constructed from cane or willow there wasn't even any heavy lifting to do. So when Angel first appeared I was, as I said, reading; *The Life and Opinions of Tristram Shandy, Gentleman.* Strangely fitting that it should be this work, antique and yet at the same time the acme of contemporaneity, which would bring us together. "How are you enjoying it?" she asked after I had inserted a railway ticket to mark my place and shut the cover. "Immensely," I replied, and we were off.

Turned out she had not just stopped in for conversation however, but was genuinely interested in a small round table with cane legs and a white melamine top. A particularly ugly piece I thought but she explained that her house was tiny and that it might serve as a dining table in her diminutive kitchen cum living room. She took measurements and returned several times over the next few days to look at it. Each time we ended up discussing literature. *Shandy* was a diversion from my normal fare at the time, consisting as it did either of nineteenth century Russians or of more contemporary English works. She advised that when I finished it I should undertake *Gulliver's Travels*, which I only knew as a children's adventure book. "No, no," she insisted, "it is much greater than that. You probably only know the first part, the Disneyfied version. Wait until you get to the philosophers who have to carry around all the objects of their discourse." So of course I did, and was thus further introduced to the archaeology of the postmodern.

Having decided to buy the table she enquired about delivery. I explained the charge and she was horrified. "But it's only around the corner; in Hay Hill." She then offered me lunch in return for my carrying it around. So my first visit was in the style of one of her Swiftean philosophers, balancing a table upside-down upon my head, thus enabling us to eat. Since she had paid in cash I had not learned her surname, "Call me Angel" being her only introduction. It seemed we were both enamoured of literary jokes and allusions.

Her house was indeed tiny, part of a small terrace that had once housed artisans or other members of the servant classes, crammed into the lane that ran between the grandeur of the Paragon and the steep ascent of Lansdown Road. I stepped down from the paved lane and was welcomed straight into a room which, since the north facing and somewhat dirty window admitted little light, evoked the subterranean lair of some nocturnal species of acquisitive mammalian creature, the exotically striped and luxuriously furred badger for example. The room was crammed with kitchen sink and stove, an over-stuffed sofa spread with oriental draperies, shelves displaying a multitude of tins and variously shaped tea caddies, others with condiments and brightly coloured spices, pans suspended from hooks, jars of upturned wooden spoons and other culinary implements, a mismatched couple of upright wooden chairs, theatrical posters pinned up to walls and, surprisingly to me, no shelves groaning under the weight of books. Merely a solitary volume lying folded open across one arm of the sofa.

We pulled the chairs up to her new acquisition, sat and talked and ate open sandwiches whilst I studied her face with its steel grey eyes whose pupils seemed to bore directly into my own, asking unvoiced questions of me, noting and possibly recording every nuance of my own expressions. Her inquisitive visage was framed by a cascade of unruly, waving dark brown hair that fell about her shoulders, and was graced by a mouth so sensuous, so full, with an under lip so pronounced it seemed it might have been bruised in some physical altercation. Possibly in moments of intense concentration she bit or chewed upon that lip, for it always appeared as if she were the possessor of a speaking wound, as if it were so infused with blood it might split or crack open at any moment.

I must have passed muster under the intensity of her scrutiny for I was invited back "whenever I felt the need." A strange turn of phrase I thought, but nevertheless I was by now totally fascinated and returned several times for what I had come to regard as a literary luncheon. Until one fateful afternoon when I just thought "Oh bugger it," and didn't bother returning to work. Instead I was taken upstairs. I can't remember what the pretext was, possibly to look something up as it was there that I found the loaded bookshelves resided, as well as the desk surmounted by an enormous electric typewriter. The significance of this eluded me at the time, distracted as I was by the flurry of discarding and discarded clothes. And afterwards, overwhelmed by my first encounter with a woman who not only knew what she wanted but was not shy in guiding me into providing it, I was too satiated to consider the implications of my surroundings. It was the following day that my unobserved clues were brought home to me.

Luckily I had not been missed, no thwarted customers had reported my absence to the parent establishment and my boss had not picked that afternoon for one of his intermittent inspections. The next morning, when a thirty-something couple were investigating the seating possibilities of our stock, she passed by outside the window, no doubt returning home from a sortie to the supermarket.

"My God, there's Angel Clare," the husband expostulated, "I was at university with her ten years ago."

"She, um, she just lives around the corner," I stuttered as, dumbfounded, I processed this piece of information. Her surname. Or rather, her nom de plume, the name under which she had written the three novels I had previously read, and a further two that I hadn't got around to yet. Oh my God, I had slept with one of my heroes, or heroines perhaps that should read. Who knew? Back then, in the early seventies, language was beginning to undergo a process of change. And Angel herself was an integral part of that transformation.

After the revelation things were different. With me, not with her. I returned a number of times, in the evenings after work. We even went out occasionally, usually to see a film at the tiny art-house cinema, for we were both classic film buffs. German expressionism was a shared passion. To sit together with a modern-day inheritor of the genre, who was also its greatest subverter, while Louise Brooks or the heavenly Marlene were illuminated on a screen, dallying with the ridiculousness of men's libidinous desires, was an education in itself. Our conversations after such screenings were always difficult for me. She knew so much, saw so much, had thought so much. With her giant intellect she was effortlessly able to reduce me to a state resembling that of a stuttering schoolboy, or indeed the humiliation of the erstwhile professor. It couldn't last, and of course it didn't.

On our last evening, after a fervid encounter thrashing about in her bed, she took me to meet a friend who lived in a nearby flat. Another novelist, a contemporary of hers whose identity now escapes me. I remember a wall of books, stacked so high that he required a wheeled library ladder to reach the upper shelves. I remember them talking, whilst I sat overwhelmed on a leather sofa in silence, an adjunct, a hanger-on of sorts, something to trot out on social occasions, the male equivalent of a handbag. It wasn't really like that of course, she wasn't that cruel. It was my own self-effacement that undermined me, my own diffidence that unmanned me. I left her that night and never returned.

Some thirty or so years later I was to remember the lessons that she had tried to teach me when first we met. Feminism had changed the world by then and the society that Angel had been carried off from was very different from the one that she had been born into. I was different too. I had long since shaken the dust of England's hierarchical streets from my feet and had finally settled, as so many immigrants before me, in one of the sun-drenched and ozone-washed suburbs of Port Adelaide, where the Lefevre Peninsula fingers out into the Gulf St. Vincent.

As is my wont, I was spending my Sunday morning fossicking amongst the towers of ill-balanced and musty-smelling second-hand books piled on Mr. Benson's stall; part of the giant weekly flea market housed in the one remaining cargo shed by the estuary on Queen's Wharf.

Out front a cacophony of amplified sounds vibrated the air, as competing skippers from the two moored pleasure cruisers touted for dolphin-spotting passengers, and a second-rate busker attempted to extricate change from the crowd with a badly rendered selection of 'classic' hits. The lighthouse was doing good business with over-excited children dragging their amused and sometimes reluctant parents inside to scale its giddying vortex. The caravans and trailers of various fast food outlets imbued the air with the cloying smell of boiling fat while queues of customers waited impatiently for their hot dogs, burgers and chips, or dim sims and other deep-fried comestibles. The fixed wooden benches and scattered plastic chairs were in great demand and the green rubbish bins were full to overflowing.

A carnival atmosphere prevailed over all, emphasised by the variety of ethnic clothing worn by perambulating family groups; by courting couples holding hands and laughing at very little; by young women with bright blue hair; or young men with enormous plastic bungs obscenely distending their ear lobes. There were numerous individuals with illuminated arms and shoulders, in either Asian, Polynesian or Celtic styles, while others sported more modern designs crawling tantalizingly up the backs of skirted thighs or, more threateningly, proclaiming a selection of trite homilies emblazoned in gothic script around their throats. The whole crowd accompanied by the screaming of gulls fighting over cast away chips or pecking at discarded plastic containers. A normal summer's Sunday morning beside the glistening Port River where, if you stared long enough, you would eventually be rewarded by the sight of a number of swept-back fins breaking the surface, as a family group of a very different species snuck past in search of their own lunchtime repast.

Inside the transformed cargo shed the atmosphere was very different. The sheer volume of air enclosed was commensurate with that within a Gothic cathedral, and pressed down similarly upon the dwarfed supplicants shuffling about and picking over the relics of other people's lives. A hundred and more stalls proffered to the curious all manner of artefact, from military medals to green glass jelly moulds, from rusty tools to fifties dresses and outmoded lingerie, from damaged furniture to trays of mismatched spoons and vinyl L.P.s of *Oklahoma* or *Herb Alpert's Christmas Album*. The windowless structure admitting of no natural light, the dim illumination provided by an inadequate number of fluorescent tubes contributed to the hushed, reverential atmosphere instilled in the minds of those seeking the soporific comfort of nostalgia.

Thinking myself immune to such a siren call I made my way directly to the overflowing tables and the precariously stacked towers of Mr. Benson's temporary emporium. There were other bookstalls in the market but none of their proprietors displayed the nicety of discrimination so evidenced by Benson's selection of predominantly literary fiction. He also stocked crime novels and a smattering of university textbooks, but none of the *National Geographics*, knitting magazines, cheap romances or *Reader's Digests* so evident on the shelves of others. If you wanted a Penguin Classic of Aristotle for example, a dog-eared *Lady Chatterley*, a Dostoyevsky, or an almost-pristine Ian McEwan then it was to Benson's that you came.

I was carefully trying to extricate a copy of Hemingway's *Men Without Women*, a collection of stories that I had not read for decades, when I pulled over the ten or so books surmounting it, causing them to fall about my feet. Apologising profusely as I retrieved and re-stacked them I was transfixed once again by Angel's face. In my trembling hands I held one of her early novels and the photograph which stared at me from the back cover must have been taken within a few years of our acquaintance; the same piercing eyes, the same cascade of unruly hair and the same pouting and determinedly sensuous under lip. In an instant I was carried away, back to that tiny house in Bath and to the period when I had stood upon my own threshold and she had proffered her education.

Straightaway I realised how much I had unconsciously taken her lessons to heart, how I had absorbed all of her dictums. I had voluntarily put myself through rehab and was now clean of everything except red wine and Chinese tea. I had travelled extensively and eventually settled in a country where, surprisingly, not only were the swans black, but all the rest of the fauna had seemed so fantastic to the early settlers that they might have hopped straight off the pages of Jonathon Swift; as if Gulliver had visited the very continent some fifty years before their own arrival. Established in my new domicile I had finally passed through the hallowed halls of academe, spent time sitting in lecture halls and, with a furtively smiling face, discussed her works on a course in post-modernist literature. I was now living with a woman with whom I seemed perfectly compatible and to my amazement my own first novel was shortly due for publication. I was older now than Angel was when she had been carried off but with a sudden laugh, which unsettled the purveyor of so much classic literature, I remembered the final piece of advice she had imparted to me, that there was simply no point in writing anything until you had something to say.

THE EMASCULATION
OF ANTHONY

"For God's sake, what *is* the matter with you?" Jen had finally shouted at him on this particular day.

"Nothing," he'd shouted back and, furious, grabbed his rod and plastic bucket of fishing gear, stormed out of the broken-down cottage and walked the short distance along Grand Junction Road to the top of West Lakes. It was low tide and the artificial lake was draining through the culvert beneath the road, flowing out into the Port River estuary, causing a series of wild curlicues to spin across its surface and disturb the sacred ibis' probing along the shoreline.

The fact was that Anthony did have a problem but was too embarrassed to mention it to his partner. They were young, barely in their twenties, and although they had lived together for a couple of years and parented a son they hadn't really talked much. Or rather he hadn't, if he were honest, not about stuff like this: feelings and...whatever. Well, you didn't, did you?

Jennifer knew that something was up, but whenever she asked he erupted with such violent, hair-trigger anger that she became wary of his fists. When he had been crook she had accepted his bad temper as just another symptom, but he had been back on his feet for more than a month now and she was thoroughly sick of tip-toeing around him.

He had been seriously ill back in the winter, almost on the point of collapse before she insisted on taking him to the G.P. He had very nearly passed out on the bus. After an hour, when they finally did get into the consulting room, the doctor very quickly diagnosed pneumonia and called for an ambulance. After starting him on a course of heavy duty antibiotics the hospital discharged him the next day; it was flu season and they needed every bed they could muster. They made Jennifer promise he would be kept warm and made to rest.

That had not been so easy. Their ramshackle little rented cottage in Portland, just south of the Port Adelaide railway station, was draughty and, in the winter, cold and damp. It was well over a hundred years old and for the last few decades had not been well looked after. The iron roof was rusty and leaked in places, the busted gutters overflowed during the slightest downpour and some of the ship-lapped boards were rotten where the paint had long-since peeled away. On top of this their child was far too young to understand that Daddy needed peace and quiet. Rather than suffering Tyler's screams and tantrums Jennifer had spent her afternoons pushing him around K-Mart, Coles and the Port Mall. Alternatively they had caught a bus to the giant Westfield shopping complex, leaving Anthony prostrated under piled-up blankets gradually sweating out his fever, or throwing them off until the shivers returned to wrack him once again.

Slowly he had recovered but it had been an expensive business. Their doctor, like so many recently, had stopped bulk-billing, so visits, even after the Medicare rebate, had cost around thirty dollars a time. He'd advised them of a radiography practice that still did bulk-bill, so at least the MRI scan that he had insisted upon was free. Not so the medicines. And, of course, two months laid up had meant that he had lost his part-time spray-painting job at the panel-beater's around the corner. His boss had been apologetic but had explained to Jennifer when she'd gone to see him that he'd been working off the books anyway, that there was a huge backlog of work, and he'd been forced to put on someone else to deal with it. He'd handed her a fifty which he'd pulled out of his wallet after scanning its contents for a few seconds and told her to get Anthony to call round when he was better.

"I can't promise anything mind, I'd have to see."

"Bugger him," was Anthony's response when she had told him. "Probably what made me ill in the first place, working there; no respirators, no extractor fans, no bloody anything. Fifty bucks? Cheapskate bastard."

That had been the longest communication that had passed his lips for a number of days and had led to a prolonged bout of coughing.

He didn't fish the estuary. It was cleaner these days but he could still remember his dad forbidding it. "You ask your grandfather about minimata disease," he'd said, "He'll soon put you straight." So he turned his back, crossed the road, dropped down onto the footpath and walked some distance around the man-made lake. The sight of all the upmarket mini-mansions which fronted the water, some with their own private landing stages, did nothing to improve his temper.

'Legoland' his Grandad Alex called it. He'd told Anthony about the area of scrubland where as a boy in the thirties he had trapped rabbits to sell to cash-strapped housewives or, for the princely sum of a few coppers, had stood look-out for the two-up schools illegally convened by furtive and desperate men. Anthony had tried hard to imagine what it must have been like, to picture the expanse of rotten marsh and wild twisted undergrowth his grandfather and his childhood mates had stalked through like intrepid early settlers. It was impossible however, and all he could do was laugh along with the old ex-wharfie at how such a derelict area had been transformed into prime desirable real estate. All he could see was the motley collection of individually designed fantasy homes clustered together like circled wagons protecting – what? He'd heard that some of them even had artificial waterfalls cascading down their living room walls.

He thought of the arrogant tosser who, one afternoon, had threatened him with the cops if he didn't move off the little jetty from which he'd been fishing. As if he was doing it any harm. Christ's sake, he'd just been trying to feed his family. Still, much as he'd felt like planting the guy he'd moved on. He had a rep for car conversion. He couldn't afford any more trouble; he had a child now, a wife, responsibilities.

Walking was uncomfortable so he didn't wander far along the circular path, just until he reached an open space between two of the houses, where he baited his hook, cast out his line and tried to get comfortable on the edge of the concrete. It wasn't easy.

He would have preferred to have been on the coast, maybe at the end of the Semaphore jetty, always had good luck there. But the walk would have been too much, and cycling was out of the question. No, the lake would have to do. It was still sea water, let in through a pipe at the southern end under the dunes when the tide was high. There was mulloway, bream and whiting in there, some said even salmon trout although Anthony had never seen one landed. A couple of whiting would do nicely for tea, would be a way of apologising to Jenny, something he knew he would have to do, something that loomed over him like an impending migraine. The onset of bad conscience. He felt guilty about shouting at her; she had enough on her plate just looking after young Tyler. His illness had worried her and now she was worried again. She was only trying to find out what was wrong. And there was something. He just didn't know how to tell her. A long-term relationship was a fairly new thing for him, partnership a novel concept, an unexplored country he was finding it difficult to negotiate.

He sat there for an hour, restlessly shifting about. It was a sun-bright day with hardly a breath of wind. The houses across from him were perfectly reflected upside-down in the untroubled water as if some alternative universe might exist down below. One which held out possibilities for him. He dismissed this fantasy by jumping up and waving his arms about in a fruitless attempt to frighten off the majestic pelican that kept cruising past. Unperturbed, the sedate creature merely turned its head to one side and eyeballed him down the length of its absurd judgemental beak as if to enquire, "Had any luck yet? Or should I come back later?" Then it turned, ruffled its folded wings just once and continued to paddle on its effortless way.

This was too much, he had endured a week or two of self-recrimination at his unjustified outbursts. He had admitted to himself that they were fuelled by cowardice, and now even animals were ridiculing him. It was time to return and unburden himself to his long suffering partner.

She was surprised by his explanation when he got home, empty-handed. Luckily Tyler was down for his nap so after making them a cup of tea, Anthony sat beside her on their threadbare sofa and, avoiding looking at her face, in a small voice began his confession:

"It's my arse, it's been itching like crazy for weeks now. It's driving me mad. I can't sit comfortably, I can't ride my bike and sometimes even walking hurts."

"Jesus Anthony, why didn't you say nothing?"

"It's not so easy, is it? Sometimes it really burns and I wipe and there's a bit of blood. I don't know what to do."

"Go to the doctor."

"We can't afford it. We haven't recovered from the pneumonia yet and it's rent day next week."

"You'll have to do something, see someone, it could be serious."

"It's just an itchy arse."

"Bloody men. Got no bloody idea. All that macho bullshit. Prefer to suffer in silence than admit that anything's wrong."

"I can't do nothing so what's the point?"

"You've got to see some...I know, that district nurse what comes to see mad Jackie next door. She lives just the other side of Grand Junction. I've seen her there when I've been walking Tyler. Chatted. Barbara she's called. Go and see her, ask her advice."

"Oh yes, just front up and tell a complete stranger 'Excuse me but my arse is on fire. Got any suggestions?' Not bloody likely."

"Why not? You helped her out that day when she'd locked the keys in her car."

"That was different. Didn't take me a couple of minutes. She's a professional, she won't be giving out free advice."

"And you used to be a professional car thief, what's the difference. Besides, anyone who could cope with that mad bitch once a week has got to be able to give you some advice."

"Yeh, but…"

"What's the worst she can do, laugh at you? I doubt it, she don't strike me as being that way."

So later he found himself standing on the veranda of a neat little cottage on Emerson Street, trying to muster the courage to knock on the door. Eventually a dog inside must have sensed his presence as it started to bark, so he was forced to carry through with it. Either that or turn and run away like a kid caught out in a stupid prank.

She seemed friendly enough when she opened her door and, recognising him as her one-time saviour, invited him inside. With the wire-haired terrier-cross sniffing at his ankles they proceeded down the narrow hall into a warm kitchen. She was obviously baking something for her evening meal but nevertheless, she ushered him through what had once been the back door into the modern extension that was her living room. From the seat he was offered on a couch he could look out through the picture window and see the light fading from her diminutive garden. She took a blue velvet armchair opposite him and raised an enquiring eyebrow.

"Look, this is a bit difficult, and I wouldn't blame you if you told me to bugger off but my wife, Jennifer, you've met her a few times I reckon, she said…" and he started to explain his problem.

She didn't laugh as he'd been expecting but she did say that he needed to see a doctor.

"I'm a nurse. I don't do private consultations."

"I know. I shouldn't have bothered you. I'd better go. It's just…" and, emboldened by her lack of derision at his predicament, he blurted out all of their straitened circumstances; his illness, the medicines, bills, the upcoming rent.

"You poor man," she said once he had unburdened himself. "Look, I was just about to pour myself a drink. Join me in a glass of wine?"

"Um, yeh, if you're sure."

He reached for the glass of red wine she poured for him and nearly quaffed it all in one go before sinking back into the sofa cushions.

He was not used to talking so personally. Now, for the second time in one day it had been necessary for him to spill his guts. Surprisingly he'd found it easier to confide in a complete stranger rather than his partner, but still, talking about such a personal area, one that since infancy he had been trained to consider dirty, as somehow *shameful*, did not come easily.

"You'd better have another," she said, reaching across to him with the bottle. "I think you are going to need it for what comes next."

"What's that?"

"You stand up, you drop your dacks, you lie on the couch facing away from me and you pull your cheeks apart."

"You must be bloody joking!" He jumped up out of his seat.

She calmly remained in hers, a wry smile playing across her face and still proffering the bottle. "Not at all. You work with cars, right? You might have a fair idea of a problem but you'd never give your diagnosis without looking at it first, am I right?"

"That's different."

"Not in the least. Going by what you've told me I have a fair idea of what's wrong and I'm pretty sure I can help you get over it. It's called pruritus ani by the way, although that's just Latin doctors' talk for itchy arse. It's one of those embarrassing conditions that loads of men suffer from but hardly anyone talks about. Well, men don't, do they?"

Looking at her suspiciously he regained his seat on the couch and held out his glass. "You reckon you can cure it?"

"No, I reckon I can tell you how you can."

"So why do you need to look at my arse?"

"There could be other causes. Piles for instance. I need to eliminate some."

"You're not winding me up?"

"Why would I? Look, Anthony, I've been a nurse for nearly forty years. I've looked up more backsides than you've had hot dinners. I'm not some lonely old pervert; I have absolutely no desire to look at any more than I have to. But because you helped me out when I was visiting your neighbour, and because your wife seems like a nice woman, and for the sake of your little boy I'm prepared to do it. So, what's it going to be?"

Not trusting himself to speak he placed his wine glass on the small coffee table, rose, turned and unzipped his fly. With a reddening face he dropped his jeans and his jocks, lay on his side on the couch and gripped his buttocks, spreading them apart. He heard the gentle sigh of her seat cushion as she rose followed by the sound of her footsteps approaching, clicking as she moved slowly across the hard, tiled floor.

He was a tough man. He was the survivor of numerous fights in his old schoolyard, and later of the odd drunken brawl around the back of a pub, yet lying there on the couch he had never experienced so much trepidation, felt so vulnerable in his whole life. He had no idea why he was afraid, he trusted she wasn't going to do anything bad to him, nevertheless he prayed that she didn't touch him, because he knew that he would flinch.

"Alright, you can get dressed now. It's as I thought. You've got thrush."

"Thrush?" As he stood and dressed, still facing away from her. "That's a woman's disease, ain't it?"

"No. Men get it too. Just in a slightly different place. The cure's the same though, live yoghurt. All the antibiotics you took for the pneumonia would have caused it. Cleaned you right out."

She went on to explain what he would have to do before wishing him well and commending herself to his wife, who she suggested might have to purchase the necessary items since he seemed so easily embarrassed.

"Panty liners!" Jen choked out when he finally arrived at home, having made a detour to the Portland Hotel on the way, desperate for a reviving pint. "You're going to have to wear panty liners?" She couldn't help herself from laughing, although she could see how mortified he was.

"It's not just me. She tells all the old boys who have it. Loads of them apparently. It's to protect my pants from the yoghurt I have to spread around the area. I'll have to eat heaps too."

"Oh, I know. Believe me I know only too well. I'm sorry. It's just the thought of you in panty liners."

"You'd better bloody well not tell anyone. Especially any of my mates. If they find out I'll give you such a bloody drubbing…"

"Don't worry love. I'll stay mum. Oops, sorry, but both of my boys in nappies. It's just too bloody funny." She broke down in laughter again. His fingers started to curl up into fists but he consciously relaxed them again, moved across and held her close.

"Thanks, love," he said, "for making me go."

"I shouldn't laugh, I'm sorry, it's just that this is like, I don't know – like some kind of 'revenge of the girlfriend'."

A SHORT WALK TO THE SEA

She came in spring. Late spring. The flowers of the miele trees had all long fallen, suburban streets no more redolent of their astringent perfume. Instead the warm honey aroma of the jacarandas, the base of each tree circled by a spreading carpet of purple blossom.

It was already hot, summer hot, and this one month before Christmas. It would be a bad fire season this year. She didn't mind the heat, it was a dry, desert heat that reminded her of home and she was dressed accordingly. The only skin exposed to public scrutiny was her high cheek-boned face, and the occasional flash of the top of an ebony foot. She took such tiny steps that they seldom emerged from beneath the blindingly coloured dress. She didn't like to expose her feet. It was her best dress and her purest white headscarf. She was on a pilgrimage, although this was not the reason that she moved so slowly up Semaphore Road.

She undertook this journey twice a year, once in spring, and then again in autumn, at no small personal cost. She welcomed the pain, however. True remembrance is always painful, not the barbeque and beer jamboree nations turn theirs into. True remembrance keeps the past alive, cleans the lens and brings tragedy sharply into focus. She didn't want to forget, but then again how could she? The phrase rang over and over in her head as she walked, the orders spewed from the mouth of the warlord, was it six years ago already? No matter, they would always be with her, tolling their eternal round, the mantra bestowed by the diabolic master: "Kill the men. Fuck the women. Take the children." Over and over. And they had, laughing as they did it, excited children playing raucous party games, egged on by over-indulgent parents.

There were men sitting outside the Exeter Hotel. One of them made a comment as she approached. She couldn't hear but she could imagine. They were drinking beer. It was ten o'clock in the morning. Perhaps they had just come off a shift or maybe it was the habit of a lifetime; they were old men, probably retired. She didn't want to pass them so she waited until the road was clear for quite some distance before stepping down off the pavement and slowly traversing first one lane and then, after another long hesitation, the other. She moved so slowly, a deliberation of footsteps, as if she were old herself. As in many ways she was. Ancient.

More comments accompanied her tentative progress. She didn't really blame them. She had a television. She had watched the reports of the outrage in Paris. She knew that any woman wearing a headscarf, however black she might be, had become an object of suspicion. It was easier for Muslim men, they laboured under no rules for everyday dress and beards were currently a fashion icon. Not her. She couldn't help but stand out like, what was the phrase, 'a sore thumb'? Strange epithet. Something to do with carpenters she'd been told. Besides she was tall, like the rest of her race, taller than most Australian men. They didn't tend to like that. She wondered whether if she had arrived when she was younger she might have made it into a netball team.

Then they would have welcomed her. She had been good at sports. Once.

There were all manner of shops along Semaphore Road: furniture stores; a picture framer's; a garden centre with sacks of compost piled up alongside, flavouring the air with an earthy scent, a promise of fertility in the hot sun; racks of discounted music C.D.s outside Mr. V's; next door the physiotherapist's. She shuddered. She had had enough of physiotherapists, and they hadn't been able to do much for her, apart from causing more pain.

She didn't look into the shop windows that she passed. She wasn't here to buy anything and she certainly didn't want to see her reflection. She knew who she was, inside, and refused to acknowledge this stumbling wreck they'd tried to turn her into. She suffered, yes, each measured footstep was painful, but she endured, she would not lie down, never again would she lie down at another's behest. Today was a special day, her eldest son's birthday, and, however long it took her, she was going to make it to the sea.

Plenty of people watched her as she passed by their windows for she was an exotic sight. Not many Africans down in the Port yet and none along the peninsula. They had mostly been settled in the Parks and spread out towards Woodville. There were occasional flare ups between their youths and those of the Vietnamese, whose second or third generation unemployed teenagers were beginning to feel territorially threatened. It was yet to reach catastrophic proportions but they all carried knives and every other year some young man's life would stupidly be pissed away over nothing, the promise of his manhood running down a gutter.

"Boys," she thought. "Stupid, stupid boys."

"Kill the men!"

Her husband had been a doctor. She was his nurse. A meeting of minds, a whirlwind romance and two sons in fairly short order. A house in the city, living with his parents, a good life, a close family, something she had always wanted. A little tense at times, of course it was; arguments over food shopping, or using too much water; but nothing serious, nothing untoward. And a built-in child minder for when she returned to work.

But her husband, Beno, had a conscience which grew and grew. Working in the hospital, patching up drunks who had fallen off motor-scooters, treating government officials with not much wrong with them and then, in the other wards, watching children die of preventable diseases, quieting the anguish of the innocent, trying to ease their passage out of the world. All the while under the reproachful stares of mute parents.

Eventually, one night, he had put to her a proposition.

"We could both get jobs with an NGO. Travel round the country a couple a years, helping the people most in need. The boys are old enough now, be good for them to see their land, get away from all this noise and pollution, experience the reality of other people's lives before they go to high school."

She had considered, then agreed, and shortly she had found herself feeding her boys from the back of a dusty Land-Rover or sharing meagre meals with village tribeswomen, whilst her husband set broken bones or cleaned up wounds, examined ears and throats, lectured mothers on hygiene. Then the pair of them would break out the needles and syringes and a mass inoculation of children would begin.

It was this that caused the problem. How were they to know that the prevention of childhood diseases, the eradication of polio and the like, was nothing but a degenerate Western plot, a ruse promulgated by the Great Satan to render Muslims infertile, prevent the glorious worldwide spread of Islam? They had no idea until the day that the technicals roared into the village, slewed around in a cloud of dust and disgorged a crowd of roaring boys who ran about, out of their skulls on khat and brandishing their AK-47s. The older men stayed on the trucks, rotating the machine guns in all directions. It seemed a plague of locusts had descended to give them the news.

Beno was the first to be shot, once all of his medicines had been smashed in front of him, and on him, and finally forced down his throat. He was not alone however, for had not all of the men been tarnished by his dangerous heresies, and did not the infection need to be cauterized? No matter that they were all of the same Muslim faith, all brothers under the skin, for sinners are required to be punished. The Flames of the Desert were here and they would mete out justice. They would certainly do that job.

There was an old man sitting in a cane chair shaded by the veranda of an antiques shop, enjoying the slight breeze that occasionally wafted down Semaphore Road from the sea. His hair had been bleached pure white by the sun and his mouth was open revealing a row of tombstone teeth too big for his jaw. She thought he was scowling at her but as she neared he looked up and asked, "Warm enough for you?"

She didn't know how to reply. She couldn't read him. Was he just being polite, passing the time of day with an amusing remark, or was it, because of her African appearance, an unpleasant dig? She had been able to speak English from the age of ten, but in the mouths of Australians the language was used in ways unknown to her schoolteachers. Her first impulse, transported as she was into a dark time in a far distant place, was to think he was attacking her ethnicity or maybe her faith. Not that she had much faith anymore; merely went through the motions. Besides she knew too well what a lot of Australians thought of their own black-skinned people. Nevertheless she chose to interpret it favourably, managed a weak smile and in a voice little more than a whisper replied, "Yes, thank you," and moved inexorably on. She was a third of the way towards her destination.

More shops, with an occasional private house mixed between them: a hairdresser's; a take-away food outlet; souvenirs and fancy homewares; an estate agent's; skate board and surf necessities; a natural-high herb shop; a florist's; restaurants; and a number of cafés where women with white fluffy dogs sat at roadside tables and lowered their voices as they observed her halting progress.

A man was perched high up a ladder outside the cinema, leaning out dangerously wide to change the letters for the coming week's attractions. She thought of the last film she had seen, *Toy Story*, outdoors under a sliver of moon and a wheel of different constellations. They had taken their sons for the first time, and the eldest had laughed so much he had cried at the wonder of it. The younger had been more interested in sliding about on the plastic seat of his collapsible fold-up chair. Had they seen the sequels?

There was another pub in the distance so she crossed the road again. It was easier this time as the traffic was slower and there was a broad grassed median strip with shade-giving trees that she didn't know the name of. There was even a bench on which a drunk man sprawled, clutching to his chest a bottle in a brown paper bag. She cut across behind it, putting plenty of space between them. She had no desire to be harangued, or begged from, or possibly attacked. She could no more run than she could raise up the dead, and she knew the effects of alcohol only too well.

On the other pavement a tall thin man in black jeans and tee-shirt placed a coffee at the elbow of a man in a straw hat. He was sitting in the shade of an orange café umbrella, studiously typing into a lap-top. After a few laughing words the tall man turned, just as she mounted the kerb. She lost her footing and stumbled. He reached out to steady her. Her foot emerged from the hem of her dress and the pair of them saw it. Her right foot.

"My God!" the seated man blurted out.

"Are you alright?" From the thin man who had grasped her as she stumbled. "Here, take a seat, rest for a moment."

"No, thank you, I'll be fine." She was embarrassed. She could not stay. They had seen her foot. She had seen their pity. She had to move on.

When she had left the man at the table asked, "Jesus, did you see that? How can she walk on a foot like that?"

"With great difficulty, I'd reckon," replied Phil, the café proprietor, as they both watched her slowly move away. "I'll tell you one thing. When I reached out for her, she flinched." The two of them looked into each other's eyes for a moment. Then Phil re-entered his establishment and the sitting man resumed tapping away at his keys.

"Fuck the women!"

She thought herself lucky in one small way; she hadn't been raped in front of her husband, for he was already dead. Not so some of the other women who were thrown to the ground and mounted where they lay. The younger, more impetuous husbands who tried to intervene were rapidly dispatched, whilst the rest were clubbed with rifle butts and prodded with barrels into a trembling group, quivering in their mixture of rage and fear, anguished and boiling with impotence.

She was taken, repeatedly, unnaturally at times, they all were, in a heaving mass of outflung limbs, of gyrating torsos, of shrieking and screaming and demoniac laughter, an orgy of adolescent lust from the slime-pits of unbridled libido. The older raiders stood by their guns and watched, mouths twisted into grins of knowing amusement, only occasionally dragging one of the younger, the prettier girls out of the heap for their own solitary pleasures. Mostly they watched the shuddering pile as the boys played out their twisted and drug-fuelled desires, for this was their reward, this was what served to keep them enslaved as boy soldiers. The power. The drugs, the guns and the power.

Next to the café was a fish and chip shop; a double row of cream-brick two-story units facing each other across a small divide; a jewellers; a newsagents with a wine bar above and after that a smallish low-slung supermarket. A car park, a library, an ice-cream parlour and a second-hand dress shop, where she froze, forced to arrest her creeping progress. She pretended to study the display of inappropriate skirts and dresses. A couple of men wearing combat fatigues had spilled out from the RSL next door. She could not pass them, her right leg would not let her; paralysed, as if it had grown straight down into the earth. The two young veterans were laughing and joking, seemingly without a care in the world. She thought she heard the phrase "rag heads" and she wondered if they were referring to her. But they couldn't have been. They were carrying on a conversation they had started inside. And besides, they walked straight over to an old rusty Datsun, slammed shut the doors and drove away. They didn't even see me, she thought.

After a few calming breaths her heart resettled and she was able to move on. It was difficult for the street sloped down quite steeply, past the Mexican restaurant and the old bluestone time-ball tower perched high on the embankment above. Going down thrust all of her weight onto her ankle and the pain increased enormously. Nearly there now, she gritted her teeth, concentrating on the white marble angel whose outstretched wings were attempting to embrace the whole of humanity from on top of its squat, grey column. She waited for the green walking man, although there was no traffic, and as she arrived at the foot of the war memorial she reached out and ran her hand across the rough granite.

It's a woman up there, she thought. Men's angels are always women and, of course, they're always white. There was no redemption in the stone-cut angel's wings though, nor yet in the laurel garland that she clutched. Rather she was diminished, a decorative flourish, like a ballerina perched upon a music box, by the four imposing clock faces displayed beneath her. Each dial was framed by a massive pair of columns supporting a classical pediment, so that they resembled time-pieces removed from giant Victorian mantle-pieces, and attached back to back to face the cardinal points. The whole monumental edifice much more fitted to a railway concourse than to any spiritual way station.

"Take the children!"

After it was over they rounded up the crying children, the boys and a few of the girls, tied them together in the semblance of a chain-gang, and lifted them onto the back of a flat-bed truck.

No! Not her boys! She had to save them. Exhausted and bloodied, crying in pain, she crawled across the ground, screaming, pleading and clutching at one of the devil's legs. Who turned, laughing, and smashed the butt of his rifle down, down, again and again onto her unprotected foot. She passed out, and when she awoke they were gone.

She had made it to the jetty, past the kiosk and the little steam train that was just pulling out from its terminus, carrying a horde of excited children packed into miniature carriages, some on laps, others held so as not to lean out too far by their equally excited parents. The driver sitting astride his model engine blew the whistle, immediately echoed by the shrieks of high-pitched voices as they made their giggling progress along the beachside track.

She picked her way carefully out along the boards, mindful that some had warped in the sun, curled up to catch at any unsuspecting foot. The tide was low and there were acres of golden sands stretching down to the gentle rippling of the azure sea. Fishers eagerly watched their rods at the far end of the jetty, or cast out baited pots in the hope and expectation of crabs. The sand was sprinkled with family groups. Grandfathers held the hands of naked tots who laughed as the wavelets splashed up their chubby little legs. Mothers lay back on towels but behind their sunglasses kept ever-watchful eyes wide open. Fathers relived their own architectural endeavours as they aided their offspring in the construction of castles, digging channels and encouraging water to flow into temporary moats. Further out older children swam or threw balls at one another as a man standing upright on a board paddled lazily past.

She surveyed this idyllic scene and wondered where her boys were now. It was her eldest's birthday today. A part of her hoped he was dead. Rather that than turned into a ravening beast, roaming the desert with other crazy zealots, inflicting unspeakable atrocities on further helpless mothers. But maybe he'd escaped. He and his sibling been rescued by government forces, been returned to what passes for a normal life. This was her fantasy, the dream that she clung to, the preservation of her sanity.

But there was no government, she knew that too well, only jumped up warlords with their gangs of vicious thugs, their grasping for power, their internecine strifes: only violence, starvation, suffering and death. And she saw how peaceful the families around her, how carefree they appeared to be.

Sure, people have troubles, she had no monopoly on suffering, she knew that too. Marriages break down in anger, there's domestic violence, unemployment, homelessness, the grinding anguish of a parent whose child is born with severe disability, accidents, all manner of strokes of fortune that manifest as the human condition. But still, in this place and at this time there was peace, the eternal consolation of the golden sands, the lulling of an ever-changing sea.

Gingerly she descended the steps from the jetty and dragged her foot across hot sand. When she arrived at the place where the land gently slipped under placid, rippling water she hitched up her dress and tucked a fold into the elastic of her knickers, as she had done so long ago when she had been but a child herself.

She stepped into the liquid's warm and kind embrace. She looked down at the miniature skittering fishes and thought how her sons would have loved to run splashing through the shallows, laughing, and trying to chase them. She saw too, with a fleeting pleasure, how the refraction of the slanting light as it bent through the water had appeared to have straightened out her foot.

A FICTION IN HISTORY

The fine-lined clipper ship with all sails neatly furled slid effort-lessly up the Port River, under tow from a double side-wheeled paddle steamer. The tide was high and the profusion of mangroves obscuring the river banks appeared to be floating in the early morning mist, indolently waving in the churned up water. Joseph watched from the forecastle as a heron stretched out its neck and launched itself from a perch amidst the leaves and then, with languid wings, glided further downstream, away from the rhythmic clanking of the little steamer and the dark smudge issuing from its smoke stack. He glanced up at the crew-men ranged along the fore-topsail yard, ready at his command to unfurl the sail should the towing hawser come adrift for any reason. Having travelled ten thousand odd miles from Plymouth with no mishap it would be ignominious to suddenly lose steerage and finish beached upon a river bank just short of their destination.

As the sun rose higher the temperature increased considerably. The mist was soon burned off and Joseph began to sweat beneath the weight of his uniform jacket. A shout from one of the passengers eagerly lining the deck disturbed him for a moment, but he was instantly reassured to see that they were merely excited by the antics of a pair of dolphins swimming alongside them. He remembered being similarly escorted into port on his previous voyage and wondered whether these could possibly be the same two creatures, delegated by some divine providence to welcome incoming vessels. He shook his head to clear the fancy of his imagination and returned to the duty of surveying the passage, on the look-out for any unexpected sand bars which might have shifted with the tides.

The rope held and eventually they entered into the port reach proper, to be granted a view of so many vessels, both at dockside and anchored out in the stream, the profusion of masts resembling a forest unseasonably denuded of leaves. Just before arriving at the heart of the port the pilot swung them leftwards, steering the vessel into the Company Basin. The swing bridge was open and they passed through the narrow channel into the New Dock, there to moor at the wharf before the magnificent building of Elder, Smith and Company, the proud and prosperous owners of their stately vessel. Joseph knew this huge and elegantly-faced building housed on its several floors thousands of compressed bales of wool, some of which would be cargo for them on their return trip to London. He reflected on the profits that must accrue from the husbandry of such an accommodating and inoffensive animal. He wondered how many men and vessels had perished over the years as they struggled to transport such a bounty to market. He stroked his fingers through his neatly trimmed beard remembering his own first voyage to the Antipodes some fifteen years before. Back then he had been an ordinary seaman receiving the meagre stipend of one shilling per month.

Once the vessel was secured, fore and aft, stevedores wheeled a gangway up to her side and the passengers began to disembark. Some of them stumbled on stepping ashore, their first faltering steps on terra firma for four months rendering them as unsure of footfall as the youngest of children. More men swarmed aboard, shirt-sleeved and hatted, with broad leather belts securing their trousers, and the unloading of luggage commenced, to be stacked alongside on the wharf. Soon horse-drawn carts pulled up to carry it, and such owners as preferred not to walk, the short distance around the corner into St. Vincent Street, to deposit their cargo at the railway station for the short journey into town.

By late afternoon, the passengers gone and what little extra cargo the vessel had carried in its hold unloaded, Joseph's duties were fulfilled. The crew had long since departed. Since the *Torrens* was held in such high regard as a lucky ship, several of them had signed on previously for her regular voyage to South Australia, and had their own favourites amongst the numerous hotels of the port. They were also keenly aware of which amongst them doubled as brothels. The skipper had also disembarked, ensconcing himself in the recently built Colac Hotel, a short step from his vessel and a favourite with visiting captains. Having detailed one of the youngest seamen to stay aboard as watchman, Joseph decided on a walk along the wharf, around the side of the Company Basin and along to McLaren Parade, beside the river proper, surveying as he went the names of the multitude of vessels tied up.

As a seaman dedicated to the romance of sail he was saddened to see the growing numbers of steam driven ships there berthed. He had had some experience on a coal-fired steamer, plying the sea routes of the Malay archipelago, and regretted what some were saying would be their inevitable ascendance. The world had changed somewhat since the opening of the Suez Canal, and further now since the development of more efficient boilers with which to power the new multiple expansion engines. They seemed to him to be clumsy, dirty affairs when compared to the clean and elegant lines of the clipper ships which proudly thrust their carved figure-heads forward beneath needle-pointed bowsprits. He was gratified to see that the steamers were still vastly outnumbered by those carrying masts and spars, but he wondered for how long.

He walked along McLaren Wharf, and paused to watch the 'Big Crane' busily unloading sacks of wheat from the hold of a neat little coastal ketch, prior to adding them to the cargo already stowed aboard a nearby barque. He recalled the iron barque *Otago* which he had commanded, and brought to this very dock for unloading four years previously. He determined to visit the offices of Simpsons, the *Otago*'s owners, to see if his acquaintance Alfred Saunders was still a clerk in their employ, so he turned to his left, passed under the giant signal mast and entered their building on Queen's Wharf. A square-faced man with rolled up shirt sleeves leapt up from a desk and thrust out his hand.

"Joseph! It's good to see you again. I saw from the *Register* that the *Torrens* was due in today and was wondering if you were on board. How are you? Good voyage, I trust."

"Fine thanks, Alfred. Except that I'm sweltering in this heat."

"No wonder. Take off your pea jacket. It can't be healthy for you."

"I would, but for the fact that as soon as I did, I fear I would soon be shivering again."

"Still suffering the old trouble?"

"Oh yes, very much so. Now that we've docked and I can relax I find I am building up for another bout. Our surgeon advised me to try and sweat the fever out."

"That's too bad. Look, if you can wait for a moment while I finish these bills of lading we'll go for a drink."

"Not sure that's advisable. I'm pretty dosed up on quinine."

"One won't hurt. It'd do you good."

Sometime later they were sitting in the snug of the Commercial Hotel exchanging their news over a couple of brandies.

"Wheat's not doing so well at the moment," explained Alfred, "but our Black Diamond Line's going from strength to strength. Coal from Newcastle is our main commodity these days. The old man is considering buying another vessel."

"Nasty, dirty cargo. And a propensity to catch fire in a hold."

"The way of the future, Joseph. Everyone needs it. Hart's flour mill down the wharf. Dunn's. The railway. The gas companies. And now all these new steam ships."

"In every port I see more and more of them. On the *Torrens* we have a crew of twenty-five men to trim the sails. How many on a steamer. Six? Soon us old sea-dogs will be left high and dry."

"You'll be safe. They'll always need ship's officers. People with authority."

"Maybe, but what about the men?"

"There'll be other jobs, new jobs. People have to move with the times. Get into coal, it's an industry that'll never die."

"I'm not sure my crew are equipped to take it on board."

"Then they'll fall by the wayside. I'm sorry Joseph, but it's commerce makes the world go round, and commerce is saying machinery. And coal."

"To increase business profits."

"Of course. Without profit there's no progress, no incentive for improvement."

"I'm not convinced it is an improvement. That's all that I'm saying. For businessmen certainly, but for the man in the street?"

"Who gives a fig for the man in the street? Maybe we should change the subject. You're a romantic and I'm a pragmatist. And never the twain shall meet. So, tell me, what else has been happening in your life. Are you married yet? I don't see a ring."

"No, no wife, although my uncle keeps suggesting that it's about time."

"And so it is. A wife would soon cure your idealism."

"That is not all that he wants. He has a friend who is a craniologist, whatever that is. And he wants me to send him some skulls."

"Skulls! People's skulls?"

"Aboriginal skulls. So they can compare and contrast them. Weigh them, measure them, estimate brain size, and whatever else it is that they do."

"Ah. We had one of those here a few years ago. Phrenologist he called himself. Gave a lecture at the Institute about bumps on prisoners' heads. Made a lot of sense to me. Some people are predisposed to commit criminal acts."

For the last few moments the potman had been hovering, bottle in hand, waiting to supply them with refills. He was a big man in a greasy leather apron, whose massive eyebrows overhung deep-sunk, fiery eyes above plump and sweaty cheeks. Unobserved by the companions he had been listening to their conversation intently, as if fascinated by the odd-looking seaman with the down-sloping eyes and the oddest of accents.

"Is there a museum in town?" Joseph was asking.

"Certainly there is, on North Terrace, adjacent to the Governor's dwelling. In fact they are just completing a new building for themselves. Why do you ask?"

"This business of the skulls. I have a letter from the Krakow Museum. I thought I'd present it and see if they could be of assistance."

"Worth a try, although they are probably busy working up their own collection."

"I cannot think of anything else I could do," said Joseph when, looking up, he caught the fervid eye of the encroaching potman and waved him away.

"One is enough for me, Alfred. I'd better get back to the *Torrens*. I'm starting to feel the shivers coming upon me."

"I think I'd better walk back with you, you aren't looking the best." So saying, he helped his friend to his feet.

"Most gracious of you, Alfred. These insidious tropical diseases keep sneaking back to haunt a man. I fear I am shortly in for a savage bout."

Joseph spent the following few days in his bed awaiting the fever's approaching crisis. When it signally failed to arrive, and desirous of settling the unwelcome affair that his uncle had laid upon him, he finally stood and meticulously brushed down his clothes, turning his cap in his hands whilst removing any residue of salt. He reached into his mahogany writing desk to find the letter which his uncle had forwarded to him. He stood for a while as if undecided, tapping the letter against the open palm of his left hand, until a glance at the embossed coat of arms on the envelope with its two crossed maces under a golden crown steeled his resolve and he left his cabin.

It was but a short step from the wharf to the railway station and, for all his misgivings about steam powered ships, he had no such qualms about the convenience of train travel. As they pulled out from the station he noticed the few houses that backed onto the line were mostly walled with corrugated iron, whereas those around the small Alberton station were more substantial stone-built edifices. The next stop was at Woodville where some two years previously he had visited the family of Henry Simpson, the owner of the barque he had once commanded. He recalled the pleasant evening he had spent there, relating his traveller's tales to the man's two eager sons and enjoying the warm hospitality of their parents. He hoped that his reception at the museum would be equally welcoming. After passing market gardens with their neat rows of vegetables, and many fields containing horses, they stopped briefly at Bowden on the outskirts of the city, then crossed the shrunken river on an iron bridge, swept past the crenelated walls and octagonal guard towers of the colony's prison, before finally pulling up at the end of the line.

Joseph made his way along the broad thoroughfare of North Terrace; passed the Parliament building; nodded a greeting to the soldier at attention outside the Governor's residence, a greeting that was not returned; then followed a high brick wall towards the Adelaide Institute on the corner of the avenue named in the Governor's honour. Here he was informed that the museum had been relocated into the Jervois building next door. At first sight of this magnificent and imposing structure Joseph stopped, quite amazed at its profusion of Romanesque arched windows, its horizontal bandings of different coloured stone and flanked by two protruding spire-topped towers. To one side, set back behind a well-watered lawn, a lower and more modest building of red-brick had been constructed. He stood before the main structure for a while, taking in the beauty of its symmetry, before nervously entering its portal.

The building housed both a library and an art gallery, with the museum crammed into a space out the back. He was directed towards the office of the director.

"Honorary Director," the man insisted as he rose from a desk cluttered with books and papers, and reached across it to shake Joseph's outstretched hand. He was a man of modest stature, with curly light-brown hair cropped close to his skull, piercing steel-grey eyes which hinted at a lively intelligence, and sporting an enormous moustache, the luxuriance of which obscured his upper lip entirely and spread out, with drooping wings, to overwhelm the modest growth tracing down his jaw-line.

Joseph stated his business as succinctly as possible, in the manner of a man reporting to a senior officer, and then proffered the letter from the Krakow Museum.

"I am sorry Mr. Korzeniowski," the man said, on slitting open the envelope with his silver desk-knife, "I am afraid that amongst my many talents linguistics is not included, and this letter is impossible for me to read."

"I could translate it for you."

"That would hardly be ethical, I fear. You say that you are a sailor, a ship's officer indeed, and I am prepared to take your word for that. But as to allowing you to walk out of my museum with a number of artefacts from our collection on the strength of a letter in some indecipherable language which, you say, comes from one of the oldest universities in Europe, I am afraid that is out of the question. I am sorry. I note the very official-looking coat of arms on the letterhead but really, I have no desire to offend you, but I couldn't possibly accede to your request. We are a relatively young institution, still in the process of establishing ourselves. I fear I would be failing in my duties as custodian if I were to relinquish any item on the say-so of the first foreign gentleman who came knocking at my door."

"I am a British citizen just as much as you."

"If that is true then I should apologise. You must understand however, that from your accent, physiognomy and demeanour, and indeed from your request, that I would naturally assume you to be Polish, or Russian, or whatever."

"I was born into the Polish nobility, sir. Now I am a master mariner in the British mercantile marine. I am equally proud of both nationalities."

"Be that as it may, my answer remains the same. However, our institution is desirous of entering into relationships with similar institutions throughout the world. We have established reciprocal arrangements with museums in the mother country as well as some in Germany. Should this Doctor Kopernicki you mentioned, a name, I have to say, more redolent of the music hall than that of a reputable scientist, should he communicate directly with us, in English, then we might be able to come to terms with him. To surrender anything on the say-so of any passing sailor would be a dereliction of my duties. Now, I am very busy so I will just say good day to you, sir."

Furious at the insulting behaviour he felt had been meted out not only to him, as a gentleman, but also to his motherland, Joseph returned to his ship, sweating profusely and in a terrible mood. There, further bad news awaited him.

"He's shot himself, sir."

It was Singer, the junior officer who rushed up to him the moment his foot touched the deck, flapping a newspaper in his face.

"What? Shot himself? Who has? What on earth are you talking about?"

"That Mr. Durell. You know, that 'passenger for his health' that was took right poorly on the voyage. It's in the *Advertiser*. Here, read it for yourself."

Joseph took the proffered newspaper and read the article on the third page of Friday's edition. It appeared that the twenty-two year old Joseph Durell had consulted a Doctor Marten, whilst staying at the York Hotel in Rundle Street, about his worsening health. The good doctor had advised that his consumption was incurable, that he was rapidly declining, and that he should return to Europe as quickly as possible if he wished to see his family again. A passage had hastily been arranged for him on a French mail steamer by one of the partners in Fowlers, a business associate of Durell's father. However the young man left a note explaining that he could not face another long sea voyage, especially since he had no expectation of arrival. He begged the forgiveness of his family and of his God and, ever thoughtful of the inconvenience of others, he had repaired to the bathroom of the hotel before placing the muzzle of his revolver in his mouth and pulling the trigger. At the inquest a verdict of suicide whilst in a state of temporary insanity, brought about by ill-health, was unanimously passed by the jury.

This news had a profound effect on Joseph. No stranger to illness or melancholia himself, he had considered it something of a duty to try to lift Durell's youthful spirits. He had failed, and now this. It was too much. He stumbled as he made towards the poop deck. He reached out and grasped Singer's shoulder.

"Only twenty-two, Singer. Not much older than you. Enjoy life while you may. Right now I'm feeling somewhat weak myself, I must get to my cabin before I fall over."

That night the full force of the fever hit. Joseph lay fully clothed on his bunk with sweat running freely from every pore in his body. His rumpled bedclothes scattered all about him where he twisted and turned as if trying to escape some maleficent presence that stalked him. Suddenly he was roused by a loud rapping on his cabin door, which swung open to reveal young Singer looking at him with sympathetic eyes.

"Sorry sir, this man insisted that he had some business with you."

With that the junior officer was shouldered aside by a huge dark figure who pushed him outside and closed the door behind him.

"Don't want nobody else hearing this, do we now," the intruder stated.

Joseph struggled to sit up, still groggy from his fevered dreams, and with a cracking voice enquired, "Do I know you?"

"No, but I knows you. You'm the bloke as wants some skulls aint' yer? I heard yer in the pub t'other day."

"Pub? What pub?" Joseph's eyes were slowly coming into focus. The dark figure bending towards him in the low ceilinged cabin did seem somehow familiar although he couldn't place him. He mustered the strength to swing his legs over the side of the bunk and tried to stand, but straightway fell back into a sitting position. The man leaned down and grabbed him under the arms, hoisting him to his feet.

"You was in the Commercial, with that Saunders. Do you want them skulls or don't yer? I know where there's plenty. Won't cost yer much. I'll take yer, in me skiff."

Joseph's fuddled brain was starting to clear somewhat and he recognised the potman who had been hovering around them in the hotel. "Yes, yes I suppose I do. My uncle you understand…"

"Don't bother me who wants them or why. I just knows where there is some and if you want 'em you gotta come right now. The tide'll be on the turn soon, an' I don't wanna be rowing all night."

Up on deck, by the orange light of the full blood-moon just rising over the distant hills, Joseph looked about for Singer but the ship appeared deserted. He thought to have a stern word with him when they returned. Meantime they moved through the cobweb of shadows cast by the rigging, over the side and along the wharf to a flight of stone steps, at the bottom of which a small rowing boat was tethered. An anaemic-looking bull terrier raised its blunt white muzzle over the bulwarks and growled as they descended but was soon silenced by a corresponding one from the potman. The man unshipped the oars and cast off the painter as Joseph tripped over various utensils stowed in the stern sheets. He flopped down onto the aft thwart, wondering where they were going and, indeed, what the hell was really happening. For a moment the cool breeze playing across the water seemed to revive him but soon he relapsed into the confusion of his dreams. Now and again he would resurface into consciousness to see the man grinning at him as he pulled vigorously at the oars, the muscles of his brawny arms bulging with every stroke.

By the time they made mid-stream the moon had risen far enough to shed its orange hue and now cast a fine effulgence over everything about them, water dripping like liquid silver from the rising blades. The man didn't talk, just grunted in his exertions as they made their way downstream, with the pale terrier standing in the prow like some ghostly figurehead pointing their way.

Joseph was awakened by the scrape of the boat running up over a sandy bottom. Now thoroughly confused, he followed the potman and his dog up past the high-tide mark and cast about for the house to which he imagined that they were making. But there was nothing. No welcoming lights, no dwellings of any description, just scrub, sand, marram-grass and the odd low, salt-burned and withered shrub. The man cast down the bundle that had been slung over his shoulder with a clattering of metal.

"Good, don't need no light," he said as he extracted a shovel from his bundle and proceeded to dig into a slight rise in the sand.

"What the devil are you doing?" shouted Joseph, as he came somewhat to his senses and an overwhelming sense of dread lifted the hairs on the back of his neck.

"Don't make no noise."

"But what…?"

"Youm'll see soon enough. They ain't deep down."

Exhausted as he was, Joseph reached out to grab for the other's arm. A low growl emanated from the bull terrier as it curled back its pink lips and bared the teeth which glistened in the moonlight. Joseph recoiled, tripped on a root and fell backwards, sprawled in the marram-grass and lost consciousness for a few moments. When he recovered the potman had finished his frenzied digging and stood by the shallow hole he had excavated.

"There's one," he said, "Come see."

Unable to muster the strength to stand Joseph crawled to the side of the depression and stared down at a partial skeleton emerging from its sandy bed. He could see the whole front of a rib-cage, a jaw protruding towards him, and a sand filled oval surmounted by two gritty circles which had once looked out upon the world.

"Beauty ain't it. This do yer?" Swinging the shovel up past his shoulder in preparation for the downswing that he imagined necessary to slice through the neck.

Drawing the last vestiges of his strength from God knows where, Joseph launched himself at the potman who, taken unawares, lost his footing and toppled headlong into the grave, dropping his shovel in the process and clawing frantically at the sides. At this the dog leapt at Joseph and fastened its bull-baiting jaws onto one of his legs. Joseph screamed and toppled backwards again but the animal held fast. Slowly the big man rose up from the grave like some subterranean apparition manifesting in the brittle moonlight and loomed threateningly over Joseph's prone body.

"What the bloody hell d'you do that for? Yer Bully, let un go."

Mercifully the dog unlocked its jaws and Joseph clutched at his wounded leg from which blood now spurted.

"I want no part of any grave-robbery," he said as he ripped off a shirtsleeve, hoisted his torn trouser leg and tied the make-shift bandage in an attempt to quench the flow.

"Where else you gonna get skulls from?"

"I was trying to get some from a museum. I thought I was going to buy some that you had in your house."

"An' if I had they'dve still come out the ground. Skulls comes off skellingtons and skellingtons comes out of graves."

"Robbing graves is not an occupation for a Christian."

"These ain't no Christians. Them're abbos. Prob'ly been 'yer for 'undreds a years. My old man showed us this place when he were teaching I how to fish. One 'a the first settlers he were, Cornish fisherman, staunch chapel Methodist. Godless 'ee called this place, so you don't need to worry 'bout that."

"They were still human beings and I want nothing to do with disturbing their last resting place."

"Proper bloody 'ypocrit you are. Happy enough to let someone else do your dirty work ain't yer? Long as you don't have to get your own hands dirty. Museums! Where you reckon they get them from? Out the bloody ground, boy."

"I'm sorry. There's been a misunderstanding. Can we go back now? My leg needs attention."

"Long as you pay we can. I figured we could get maybe eight skulls 'ere an I were going to charge 'ee 'alf crown each. Plus ferry costs, thrupence each way. Tha's one pound six pence to my reckonin'. Pay up an' I'll take 'ec back. Otherwise you can bloody well swim. Or else lose yoursen walking this bank f'rever."

"Fine, fine. Just get me back to my ship. I'll pay you there."

"How do I know I can trust yer?"

"I'm a gentleman."

"Oh yes. A proper gennleman who just 'appens to want some dead people's 'eads."

"Please, I swear I'll pay you, but first, could you cover… that…up again."

"I s'pose you must be a gennleman. Proper soft-'earted ain't yer? Ol right."

When he had completed this task the potman gathered Joseph up into his arms as if he were a weak and helpless child, deposited him in the aft of the boat before shoving off and taking up the oars again. The injured man retreated from consciousness and remembered little of the subsequent journey back across the ghostly waters.

Joseph awoke with sun shining on his face through the porthole of his cabin. The crisis had passed and the fever had left him. Still weak, for he hadn't eaten anything for several days, he gradually stumbled out of bed. One of his trouser legs had risen up and was wound tightly around his lower thigh. Remembering his previous night's ordeal he reached down to unwind the temporary bandage and survey the wound. There *was* no bandage. Indeed, no bite marks disfigured the flesh on either leg. Moreover, both sleeves were still firmly attached to the sweat-ridden shirt that he had slept in for he couldn't remember how long. He breathed a short sigh of relief and shook his fuddled head to clear it of the disturbance of dreams. There was one singular oddity though, for when he next came to check the wallet in his locker he found that although it still contained his pound note, the one silver sixpence that he was certain had been there was gone.

The following morning he arranged a trip up into the hills, there to meet up with William Jacques, the passenger who had lent him his copy of *Madame Bovary* to read on the voyage out.

Together they spent a few days walking through the cool of the forests, both of them attempting to recover their health.

During the return voyage on the great circle route, Joseph made two new friends. These were Edward Sanderson and the novelist John Galsworthy, to whom he had shown the manuscript he had been working on sporadically for a couple of years. They had complimented it but advised that he should Anglicize his surname if he wished to see it published. He wondered what they thought of Conrad as a name.

"Joseph Conrad. Yes, it has a certain ring to it," Galsworthy replied.

The three of them would often spend the hours of his dogwatches standing together on the poop deck, while he regaled them with stories of his sea-faring life. They, in turn, told of their failed attempt to meet up with Robert Louis Stevenson on the little demesne he had established for himself on one of the Samoan islands. One night, having discussed between them Stevenson's story of *The Body-Snatcher*, he told them of his own fevered grave-robbing experience. Out of embarrassment, or perhaps from a sailor's superstition, he omitted any mention of the missing silver sixpence. He didn't want them bringing to mind the coin traditionally placed upon a dead man's tongue, as payment for the ferryman across the River Styx.

GREENLAND

"It's raining in Greenland," my son Michael says, as he bounces out into the garden where I am sitting, enjoying my early evening gin and tonic. He has probably been chased out of the kitchen by his mother.

"Lucky them. I wish *I* didn't have to water every day." It has been the driest January on record. It just didn't rain. And here we are, nearly the end of February already and still nothing.

"You don't understand," he says. "It's the middle of winter up there. It should be snowing. I was listening to this program on the radio and they said..."

I am proud of our son, as well as worried for him. His voice is wavering, overcharged not just by his current enthusiasm but also by the hormones that struggle for equilibrium within his burgeoning frame. Yet he is an avid Radio National listener. At the age of twelve he discovered the afternoon repeats of Philip Adams's night-time show. Now every afternoon when he returns from school he tunes in religiously to that gruff avuncular voice. Last night I wrote to the veteran broadcaster, informed him of the devoted acolyte who is some seventy years his junior. I am sure that he'll be chuffed. I am hoping he will award his youngest ever listener his mythical koala stamp over the airwaves, which I know would make not just Michael's day, but probably his whole year.

"It's really serious, this scientist said…"

It's serious alright, I only need to look around me. The water tank rings hollower each time I tap it, and after a day sweltering under the South Australian sun the parched and brittle soil needs longer and longer under the sprinkler to sustain the viability of our plants.

The word soil is a misnomer. For all of the compost and mulch that I have heaped upon it over the years, deep-down it is still essentially sand, so water goes straight through. The whole of the Lefevre Peninsula, which points north like a crooked finger between the sea and the Port River estuary, is one big sand spit formed by long-shore drift. Over time this current has dragged as many grains of sand as there are stars in the night-time sky up from the southern beaches, and pushed the river mouth further and further up the coast. Maybe for as long as it took to form the ice-sheet over Greenland. A geological amount of time.

I couldn't survive without my garden. For me it is a lush, green and peaceful oasis set amongst the desert of my working days. A place to sit and contemplate the beauty of the natural world. Small but completely private, surrounded on three sides by two metre high fences, and accessible only through the ranch slider from within the house. Before the birth of Michael, Mary and I would sit out here like Adam and Eve, enjoying life, as they used to say, in a state of nature. And then, for a while, the three of us, once I had erected a shade cloth tent to protect his tender new-formed flesh from a blistering by the sun. We conformed to society's norms once he had commenced at day-care and started having little friends to visit, but when he finally leaves the nest, hopefully after university, I gleefully anticipate our return, no matter how wrinkly we might by then be.

"When it rains it turns the surface of the ice black..."

I wouldn't describe myself as a gardener. What I am is an engineer, involved in industrial processes. My days are spent in the company of hard surfaces, loud noises, fire, heat, and incandescent showers of sparks. Sure, I am mostly in an office in front of drawing boards and computers, but beyond the flimsy partitions we are dwarfed like so many intruders into a kingdom of giants. Hephaestus' forge no less. Here, in huge barns on a bank of the Port River, we construct air-warfare destroyers, and service the submarines that we built. So ironic to be doing so cheek by flipper with some of nature's most perfect submariners, in the one city in the world that counts a pod of bottle-nosed dolphins amongst its inhabitants. Maybe there are further lessons to learn from them beyond mere buoyancy quotients or echo-location systems. They were land-based mammals themselves once who, a million or so years ago while we still leaped amongst the trees, were forced by changing circumstance to go back to the sea. However long it took them they learned to adapt, and returned to the mother of us all.

"And the black surface means the ice absorbs more heat from the sun, so..."

It is not just the vibrancy of the different colours amongst the flower beds, sprouting from terracotta pots and dangling from hanging baskets that entices me. It is also the scents wafting upon the gentlest of breezes as I recline, glass in hand, upon the cushions in my garden chair. Behind me a buddleia exudes a warm honey odour. The gardenias spread a sultrier, Deep South perfume from the pots that flank the open sliding door. The frangipanis continue to unwind their ice-cream blossoms and bring to mind not only the burning of incense sticks but also our occasional family holidays, our visits to Balinese temples. The marigolds, which glow in burnished fields of gold high up in those Balinese hills, here exhibit the whole spectrum from yellow to red, and give off such a clean aroma when picked, that I'm reminded of the lemony polish my mother used upon the Baltic floorboards of home.

"They reckon the whole area up there is warming twice as fast as the rest of the planet, which explains why..."

As well as the pleasure afforded by the myriad of colours and a miasma of scents is the delight I take from the visitation of birds. A delight I am glad to say is also felt by my son, who once composed a list of all the different species that he had noted visiting. The clockwork marching toys which masquerade as spotted turtle doves afford us endless amusement. They browse upon the alyssum when we have forgotten to fill their feeding tray, or plop their plump and self-important selves down into the water bowl for an impromptu bath. This is taken over each evening by frantic gangs of New Holland honey-eaters, who perch upon its sides to take their turns, shouting and shrieking with glee like young girls at a swimming pool. One by one they leap in and straight out, fluttering their wings and twitching their feathers in unashamed bliss.

The blackbirds, who in the spring dropped liquid sound all around us as they vied to attract their mates, now hop about the place, beaks stuffed with grapes stolen from the vine which drapes the gazebo, or tossing top-soil out of flower beds in their search for more animate flesh. And then there are the sparrows, little clowning acrobats, careful not to antagonise the doves at the feeding bowl, avoiding the snapping beak of a honey-eater if they come too close to an hibiscus blossom, and who at present are hanging upside-down wrenching sunflower seeds out of drooping flower-heads.

"Do you know how high above sea level we are here, Dad?"

Ah, I was worried we were heading in this direction; was hoping to avoid this question. I really don't want him to start having bad dreams, so I exaggerate a little, "Oh, about four or five metres I reckon." I know for a fact we are two metres above normal high tide level, but several times since we have lived here both ends of the humped-back Birkenhead Bridge have been swamped by king tides.

"This scientist said that there is so much water in the Greenland ice-sheet that if it goes on melting like it is then sea levels all over the world would go up by seven metres..."

Shit.

"...And then there's Antarctica. If it starts to rain down there it could all happen really quickly. In like maybe the next twenty years. We would have to move, wouldn't we, Dad?"

I can see that he's really disturbed. "It's not going to get to that, son. Somebody will come along to fix things up."

"I don't want to move, Dad."

"Neither do I, Michael. Nor does your mother. Don't worry. We are not going anywhere."

Somewhat reassured Michael returns inside and I relax back into my cushions and take a big swallow of my gin. I close my eyes and picture the house and garden under several metres of water. Dolphins are nosing through the rooms, effortlessly slipping in through windows and turning on their sides to curl around the doorways. They drape themselves in the curtains and nibble at bedclothes with their beaks. In the garden the plants wave around like seaweed, where shoals of frightened fish are desperate to hide.

I jerk awake when my son comes out to call me in for tea. I am haunted by an image from my own childhood. A recruitment poster they must have shown us in history class. A man sits in an armchair with his daughter on his knee while his son plays with toy soldiers around his feet. She looks up from the book she's reading and asks, "What did you do in the Great War, Daddy?" The man does not look comfortable.

As I stand I reach out and put my arm around Michael's thin shoulders. If we are cast out from our garden then I fear for my son.

THE NEW FENCE

The first time I met Shane I very nearly killed him. I turned off the road into the lane at the back of our new house and almost collected him with the front bumper. Luckily it had been dry for days so the brakes gripped, rather than skidding across the undergrowth propelling me into his unprotected back. He straightened up real fast and jumped to one side, then turned and offered me an apologetic smile, as if he had been the one at fault. I could see he was a bit shaken up. So was I. Then I wondered why he was out there wearing bright yellow washing up gloves, gumboots, thick jeans, and a leather jacket. I mean even though it was 5.30 it was still hot.

I should explain that this weed infested piece of waste-land is the last remnant of the old night-cart lane which once ran the whole length of the block behind the houses of Gunn Street. Now it only runs along the back of our place before terminating at the next door neighbour's high fence. Our house faces Gunn but is on the corner with Levi Street so the lane separates my back garden from the side of Shane's place. Not that I knew his name then. As yet we hadn't spoken.

Although we had introduced ourselves to our Gunn Street neighbours as soon as we took possession of our old worker's cottage, to be honest I had been a little nervous about approaching Shane and the old guy who lives there with him. Neal and

Theresa are our kind of people; he works in IT and his wife is an accountant. They invited us in for a glass of wine our first weekend and, having lived there for ten years, happily filled us in on the benefits of the locality; the proximity to the beach, the new walking track around the inner harbour and the profusion of cafés and take-away food outlets on Semaphore Road. They also warned us not to accept any fish from people who did their angling in the Port River. Dolphin calves still regularly die they told us, although they did point out that since the soda ash plant went bankrupt the pollution has somewhat diminished. I hear them leaving for work separately in their two cars in the mornings, about the same time as I do. Susie, my wife, is a nurse so leaves at all times of the day or night.

By contrast the Levi neighbours looked pretty rough, the sort of working-class native Portonians that my co-workers laughingly warned me about when they learned where I had bought. Particularly Michael. He made the usual kind of mean-spirited jokes about in-breeding, about finding my car up on bricks minus its wheels and so on. Port Adelaide still has that kind of reputation amongst city dwellers. Bloody Crows fans. I pointed out to Michael that any thieves round here worth their salt were more likely to travel to his more affluent suburb where the pickings were undoubtedly richer. That shut him up. I do feel like a bit of an interloper though, same as Neil and Theresa and many others who have moved out here since manufacturing bombed, lured by the attractively traditional but relatively cheap housing in close proximity to such a glorious beach. Gentrification they call it, although I hardly think of myself as gentry. Shane and the old guy might though. Maybe worse.

Neither of them seem to work. The old guy always wears a grubby orange boiler suit but must be well past retirement age. Very little of his tanned and stretched leather skin shows above the enormous shovel of grey beard, so that with his cascading shoulder-length grizzled locks he resembles some Biblical patriarch of indeterminate age. By contrast Shane is pasty-faced, and looks to be in his mid-thirties. In the mornings if the weather's fine I often see the pair of them sunk into the busted sofa slowly disintegrating on their front verandah as I drive out, usually with cans of VB in their hands. At least they're up, I sometimes think, not lounging in bed like total no-hopers. I always wave and they raise their cans in response but I had not yet mustered the courage to speak to them.

Now I absolutely had to. You can't nearly knock a neighbour over and ignore it just as you can't drive away from the scene of an accident, or pass by on the other side. Not if you want to maintain cordial relations that is. So, once I had navigated my way onto the hard standing of my carport, I returned to introduce myself and apologise for the scare I'd given him. I remember being surprised by the softness of his handshake once he'd pulled off a rubber glove. Terrible the stereotypes we automatically place people in. There was a bit of a smell that came off him though. I put that down to sweat and the odd clothes the dark-haired and nervous looking little bloke was wearing.

So now I knew he was called Shane and the old guy was Brian. It surprised me that they were not related. Apparently Brian had been a good mate of Shane's father. They had been shipmates in the merchant navy and later worked together on the tugs.

"Dad's dead, now Brian looks after me," he said. I didn't ask.

I did ask what he was doing though.

"Weeding. I do the lane every few months. Gets me out the house. Bit of fresh air. 'Sides, we keep chickens."

"Yes, I thought I'd heard them. So?"

"If you keep chooks you've got feed. If you've got feed you gets rats. If you gets rats you might get snakes after them. Weeds out here grows real fast, dunno why, maybe 'cos of the old night carts, you know slopping stuff around, real fertile this soil. So I keep it down to discourage 'em. Brown snakes we get round here, plenty down in the sand dunes, but they come up through the road drains sometimes, bloody poisonous bastards. Wouldn't want them coming indoors."

"Too right, Susie would go apeshit. So, good on you."

"Not the only reason, though," and he grinned and gave me a covert sort of a wink, as if he had a secret to impart which he wished me to guess. I had no idea of course, so just encouraged him with a quizzical lift of an eyebrow.

"See these ones," pointing to a particularly tall weed with palmate leaves, "know what they are?"

"Nope. Not a clue."

"Castor oil. Just about the most poisonous plant in Aus."

"Really? My mum used to give me teaspoons of that when I was a kid. Tasted bloody poisonous too."

"Alright once it's been processed, ain't it? But raw, s' bloody dangerous. Every bit of it's bad. 'S why I'm wearing gloves, but the worst part is these spikey little green fruits they get what has the seeds inside. Look a bit like wrinkly little apples covered in vicious spikes. And o'course kids want to play with 'em, just

169

can't resist can they, poor little bleeders? Stick one of them in their mouths and they're bloody dead. So I cut 'em back before they form."

"Bloody hell. I thought it was just the spiders, the snakes and the sharks you had to look out for."

"Oh no, plenty of poisonous plants about. And not just weeds neither, people grow some in their gardens, bloody idiots. Laburnum seeds is bad, and them oleanders down by the railway tracks, all sorts. It's a tough country this for kids. Just naturally curious, ain't they? See a hole they just have to poke a stick into it, never thinking what they might stir up. Got no fear see, little blighters."

My stomach growled and the smell coming off him was getting worse, not really like body odour, more caustic some-how, like burning metal. So I commended him for his efforts and went inside to start making tea, wondering all the time about the strange little fellow and his horticultural concerns.

Susie was on nights that week so it was up to me to cook. That way she has something to eat before she leaves. The smell of Indian spices must have awakened her. When she emerged, blonde hair tousled and rubbing sleep from her eyes, she looked so bloody gorgeous that I silently cursed the shift system. We'd not been married long. Still, it helped to pay for our very own first house together.

Chicken curry for breakfast must seem a little strange, but it's my go-to meal and she's never complained yet. It has to be better than the MacDonald's crap some of her colleagues have. Sitting at the table in our diminutive kitchen I told her about my conversation with Shane and the smell that came off him.

"Sounds like psych drugs," she said, "I could probably find out from someone at work if you like."

"That doesn't sound fair, spying on the neighbours."

"It's good to know who you're living next to, just in case."

"No, he's inoffensive enough. A bit weird perhaps. If he's got troubles it's none of our business to pry."

"Fair enough. It's good of him to cut down the weeds. We get enough kids who've swallowed bits of Lego, we don't need poisonings too."

So that was where we left it. I didn't mention the snakes. She freaks out at the slugs that sometimes slide across the tiles in the bathroom, snakes would be beyond the pale. We kissed, she brushed off my amorous hands with a grin, and left for her shift at the Queen Liz.

I didn't get to talk to Shane again for a few months but felt better about being on a nodding acquaintance with the pair of them as I drove past their place in the mornings. Occasionally I would see Brian struggling home from the supermarket in the Port laden down with shopping bags. If I was returning myself I would stop and offer him a lift for which he was always grateful. Conversation in the car was a little stilted, usually confined to the Power's chances of reaching the Grand Final if it was footy season. Cricket if it wasn't. Sport the great leveller, although I got the impression that he was as disinterested as I was. I wondered why Shane was never helping him, but Brian just said that his housemate didn't feel comfortable in crowds. I didn't pry further.

One afternoon I was out in my back garden digging up a scrubby patch of grass so that I could plant a flower bed. The previous owner hadn't been much of a gardener. He must have dismantled an engine out there because there were some bald patches that felt a bit oily. What with the carport, and the old tin shed that backed onto the lane and probably once housed the dunny, there wasn't a great deal of spare land out back. With the enthusiasm of the new home owner I was attempting to transform it into a pleasant place to sit of an evening where we could quaff a glass or two of wine, watch some tomato vines gradually coming into fruit and generally smell the roses, or whatever we decided to plant.

Being on the peninsula means that the ground is really sandy, not the heavy reactive clay they get further inland which cracks walls with the changing of the seasons. Whoever wrote that bit in the Bible didn't live round here! Sand is fine, just takes a fair bit of watering. Even so digging it over was fairly heavy going for a man who mostly spends his working hours in front of a computer. So I was leaning on my shovel in traditional council worker fashion when suddenly there was a rattling of stones against the rusting tin shed and a cacophony of shouting voices.

"Bloody kids," I thought, "using my shed for target practice." Incensed, I rushed across, threw up the roller door of the carport and strode out into the lane, ready to blast them with a piece of my mind.

I was unprepared for the sight before me. Shane was backed into the far corner, dressed in his usual bizarre and mismatched clothing, cowering from a hail of stones launched at him by three eleven or twelve-year-old kids standing in the street.

"What the fuck are you doing?" I cried out as I advanced on them.

Two of them had the grace to look abashed as they retreated from me but the oldest-looking one of the trio, the ringleader I assumed, stood his ground.

"Do you know you're living next door to a paedophile?" he shouted back at me, all swagger and bravado.

"Don't talk bloody rubbish," I retorted and continued to advance on him.

"That's what my dad says anyway!" he called back as he turned and fled before my onslaught, not so brave now that his two mates had left him standing alone.

"Well, he's a bloody idiot" I shouted after him.

I turned to Shane and saw that he had a cut above his left eye where one of their missiles had connected. He appeared to be on the verge of tears. "Are you alright?" I enquired but was not granted an answer. Seeing that his tormentors had gone he rushed past me, bent over, half-crouching like a wounded duck, as he ran out into the street, turned and disappeared into the safety of his house.

I was left there, fuming, and pondering on how nasty young kids can be when confronted by difference. I had my own nightmare memories of bullying in the schoolyard when my physically inclined contemporaries found out I was more interested in books than in sports. Shane was just a scared, weird little guy who didn't get out in the sun enough. He dressed a little strangely, his eyes seemed a bit too close together, he had a dark mono-brow under a low forehead and his greasy hair was probably cut by Brian under a pudding bowl in their kitchen, but that didn't make him fair game for persecution. We all have our personal idiosyncrasies, some of us are just a bit more equipped to disguise them.

The District Nurse was around changing the dressings on my arms and back when we heard the ruckus in the lane. These old tin-walled houses you can hear everything. If it was my place I'd take the sarking off and put insulation in. Still, I'm a bit past that now.

"What on earth, Brian?" Barbara raised her head for a moment but carried on with her bandaging as if it was nothing important. I was desperate to get out there because I had a fair idea what was going on. It had happened before. She wouldn't let me stand up though, got time pressures, haven't they? Twenty minutes a visit once she told me, although she didn't seem to be too fussed. Then I heard the new neighbour chase the little shits off, thank God. Next the front door flung back and we had a fleeting glimpse of Shane as he made a dash for his room. He slammed his bedroom door and I could hear his bolts being shot across. He's got quite a few, the poor little sod.

Ahh, now she's slipping the needle in. Bloody artist with a needle is Barbara, not like some of the younger ones, leave you with a bruise.

It's going to take me hours to coax him out of there once she's gone. It was because of her that he'd gone outdoors in the first place. Don't like strangers in the place, jumpy as a cat he is, and Barbara the nicest of all the nurses they send round for me. Always ready for a bit of a laugh and a joke. Not afraid of a grumpy old bastard like me, neither. You can see it in the eyes of some of them. Treat me like I'm some kind of relic from a bygone age. Which I suppose I am. Not many of us left these days – the true believers. The betrayed ones, more like.

God knows how he's going to cope when I've gone. Which, according to the quacks ain't going to be that long. Worked outdoors all me bloody life, healthy it was supposed to be them days; get out in the sunshine, breath in the sea air, all that. Get twice as much sunshine reflected off the water. No one told us about melanomas back then. Same as those asbestos blokes. If you're a working man they keep you ignorant so they can shaft you. Unions not up to much anymore, been well and truly fucked over by successive governments.

There was a time when globalisation meant universal brotherhood. Not anymore. Now it's exploit any poor bastard you can. The Chinese use slave labour in prisons? Great, they can make our jeans for us. Bangladeshis got no health and safety regulations? Great, they get the T-shirts. So what if a thousand burn to death in a factory fire? Bloody multi-nationals rule because governments kowtow to them. Labor Party still calls itself socialist. That's a laugh. Full of bloody lawyers desperate to become members of parliament, get on their own little gravy trains.

Barbara knows. She's a nurse. Knows all about long hours for little pay. The most important people in our society get the least wages. Why is that? It all goes to film stars and sports people. What good have they ever done for anyone? Bread and circuses, same as always. Those Romans knew all about it. No one reads Juvenal any more 'cepting me. Long nights on the deck of a ship, that's a bloody education, read anything you can get. "Ill met by moonlight," as you run up the coast to Jakarta or Singapore.

Bring back communism, that's what I say. Even if it's got no chance it might put a scare into those complacent arseholes who say everything they do is for the good of the country. For themselves more like. God, me and the comrades used to have some good times back in the day. Me, Bill, Alex and the rest painting all them anti-war slogans on the Birkenhead Bridge. Listening to Paul Robeson singing in the Waterside Workers' Hall. Most of them down in the ground now. Be joining them soon, I reckon.

She's packing up her kit now. Wonder if I could get her to help me out onto the front verandah, we could stand out there and sing a chorus or two of the Internationale, that'd stir up the neighbourhood.

'Cept some uptight bastard would complain. Most of them probably wouldn't even recognise the tune. Probably think it's some footy club song.

So bloody tired, better lie down for a bit. I'll get him out later, promise to cook him spaghetti and sausages, that'll do it.

I strode back into the garden and slammed down the roller door. Bloody kids, probably didn't even know what the word meant. Paedophilia, the current terror stalking the suburbs. I was reminded of a news item from a few years back. Some idiots in South Wales had burnt down the offices of a doctor unwitting enough to put Paediatrician on his brass name plate.

I grabbed a beer from inside the house and went back out to sit in one of the green plastic garden chairs to think. I was troubled. My would-be flower bed remained half-dug and the spade standing upright in the earthed-up soil made me think of a grave under construction. Those children had started a worm boring inexorably through my consciousness. I had shouted them down unthinkingly, automatically, to protect my scared neighbour from what looked to be an unreasonable assault. But what if they were right? I didn't know him, knew nothing at all of his history. Just that he was a bit of a strange character, a weird little man who was frightened to go out into the world. Was this the reason perhaps? Was he the modern anathema, the dark man set apart, the creature contemporary society considered deserving of a stoning? And how did I feel about that?

I was a recently married man who had just bought his first house. A homemaker in the process of turning it into the safe and comfortable nest in which he and his partner, in due time, would hopefully be bringing up offspring. It was inherent on me to protect that nest against any possible threat of danger. And this was the worst kind of peril that I could imagine.

My mind was in a turmoil. It was all so speculative. The word of a stupid and vindictive little kid merely relaying the overheard prejudices of his equally ignorant parent. Should I tell my wife? Wouldn't that just help to spread the rumour? Become the kind of person I despised; entering a path that would inevitably lead to a vigilante mentality?

Of course there was no proof. How could there be? Isn't there supposed to be some kind of register? I doubted that the cops would release that information even if there was one.

The smell he gave off might be the effect of whatever drugs they give to effect chemical castration. Hiding away might be to remove himself from temptation. But then again maybe he was just a frightened agoraphobic, taking psych drugs to relieve a heavy depression. The swirling vortex of sordid thoughts was getting me nowhere. All I could do was to watch and try to glean some clues. If Brian was some kind of minder then he might let something slip at some point. And if he did what would I do then? Well, at least I would know. The worst thing was the wondering, the fear. I turned on the sprinkler and walked back inside to open another beer.

❧

Come back Barbara, for Christ's sake. It's time for another shot. If I went into palliative care I could have a pump and dose myself whenever necessary. But I need to stay with Shane for as long as possible. Promised his old man on his deathbed. You don't renege on a promise to a mate. Comrades look out for each other. Who'd have thought old Bill would have such a specimen for a son.

Come on Barbara, bloody hell it hurts! Think, think…

Something wrong in the genes there. Bill reckoned it was the napalm accident when they were unloading at Vung Tau. Good job the union blacked it. God we had some power then. Unity is strength. The fuss when the blokes walked off the Jeparit! If you've got principles you've got to stick by them whatever the bloody press calls you.

Think, think…

Bloody badge of honour being called lackeys by them bastards – talk about the pot and the bloody kettle. 'Un-Australian' my fucking arse. Don't suppose that young guy next door's ever heard of the Jeparit. Or the Boonaroo. Or the shit-storm when the wharfies refused to load them. And we were right, weren't we? All them boys killed for fuck all.

Not to mention the Vietnamese. Carpet bombing. Jesus! That's a bloody war crime if ever there was one.

Bloke next door's alright, I reckon. Good of him. Perhaps he'll keep an eye out for the poor bastard.

Thank Christ, she's here.

"Come on in, love! Door's not locked!"

❧

Ever since we bought the place I had been thinking about trying to gain possession of the lane. All the other neighbours further down our block on Gunn must have done so some time once mains sewage was laid on. Now it's just a remnant from a previous life. Currently my rickety carport is the only thing that opens onto the lane and the severe left-hand turn is difficult to negotiate. If I acquired the extra yardage I could build a decent garage that opened directly onto Levi and also extend our back garden. Susie was keen too, she fancied creating a proper veggie patch out there. It would also increase the value of our property quite a bit.

So I wrote to the council. Who told me first I'd have to get the agreement of all of our neighbours. As I'd thought, Neil and Theresa were fine. I wasn't sure how the others were going to take it but thought that this would be a perfect opportunity to try and find out a bit more about them. More particularly about Shane. So one Friday after work I called round to sound them out.

They were ensconced on the sofa on their verandah. Shane leapt up to offer me his place whilst he dragged over an inverted milk crate for himself. Brian reached down beside the arm and offered me a beer from the esky he had down there. After a bit of prevarication I asked him what he thought.

"Not up to me, not my place, you'll have to ask Shane." That surprised me. I had always imagined he had taken Shane in, but the house turned out to have belonged to the dead father. His last request had been that Brian move in and look after his rather damaged offspring. Which he, as a fellow member of the Seaman's Union, not to mention the old CPA, had been more than willing to do.

"We'll need a new fence," was all that Shane said. This was true, the fence on their side of the lane was an old, broken down post and rail affair, with scraps of old rusty tin as infill between the posts. Probably the original fence from when their house was built, nearly a hundred years previously. "Can't afford it," he added.

I'd already figured that. Brian had to be on the pension and Shane must have been on some kind of disability or sickness benefit.

"Don't worry about that, we'll pay for it. What kind of fence do you want?"

"A bloody great big one," Shane immediately responded. "A tall tin job, so no one can climb over."

"That's fine," I said, "tall is good. We'll want a bit of privacy ourselves."

It was as if he didn't hear me. "Tall," he repeated. "So no one can get in."

"Any particular colour you want?"

"Tall, we'll be safe then," he repeated again.

Brian jogged my arm. "Colour don't matter, don't bother asking, whatever you like, as long as it's good and tall he'll be happy. So he can feel safe, that's all he'll care. He needs to feel safe."

I was gratified by their agreement although this didn't get me any further with my ulterior concern. In order to separate them and perhaps have a private word with Brian I asked if I could see their chooks. It was Shane who leapt up and offered to show me however. Rather than going through the house, he lead me around the side furthest from our place, unlocked a solid wooden gate and ushered me past the tall corrugated fence into their back garden. This consisted of a square of perfectly manicured grass cut so close to the ground that no interloper could slither across on its way to the chicken coop unobserved. The coop itself was to one side behind a cyclone wire fence where a trio of silkie bantams were scratching up the bare earth. What with their white feathered top-knots bobbing up and down, and the jerking of their floppy feathered legs these looked something like miniature yetis or some other unnamed escapees from Noah's ark. I pretended interest whilst Shane was much more concerned with the dilapidated post and rail job which separated us from the lane in question.

"Tall, like the one on the other side and the one at the back. That's what we'll want. Then we'll be totally enclosed. Safe."

He'd be safe alright. The corrugated iron fences on the other two sides must have been nearly two metres tall. With a similar new fence and the house sealing off the remaining border there would be a perfect enclosed quadrangle, something like an old western fort, or a walled monastery garden. I expressed my admiration for the neatness of the yard and for the accommodation of their chooks before we returned to the front of the house.

Permission granted and council paid, I arranged for the builders to come. The day before Shane and I grubbed up the old rotten posts, rolled up the rusty wire and disposed of the old tin. He was excited and we worked well in partnership. I was starting to overcome my suspicions. I was still curious but couldn't bring myself to ask why he wasn't working. We didn't have that kind of relationship. I did take a six-pack around when we'd finished. Brian looked like shit, he had obviously been a big man in his day but was now starting to look hollowed out somehow. I didn't ask.

Three weeks after the garage went up and the new fence was erected Brian died. Shane came round to our front door to tell me. To ask me if I would go with him to scatter the ashes. All his long life Brian had had a relationship with the river and the sea, firstly as a crewman on merchant vessels leaving the port and later on the tugs bringing them back in. It turned out he was a well-respected elder statesman of the seafaring community and his wish to be scattered on the river as the tide was ebbing was going to be enabled by one of the current tug crews.

"They don't like me," said Shane. "Big, scary men."

"Doesn't he have any other family who could do it?"

"Not any more. Brian said you were alright. That you'd help me."

"You'd talked about this?"

"Oh yes. He knew he was going soon. Got everything arranged. Knew I'd need someone else with me. Reckoned you'd do it, said you'd got a conscience."

I could see he'd been crying. He looked so pathetic, standing there with his red-rimmed eyes, his greasy hair and his chewed fingernails, and giving off his acrid stink of desperation.

Whatever or whoever he was, possibly the only friend he had had in his personal vale of tears had abandoned him to a life of loneliness. He was reaching out in his despondency to the only person he could think of who might be prepared to stand by him. I was under no obligation, I hardly knew either of them, but I'm not the sort of person to kick a wounded animal. I couldn't imagine the courage that he had had to muster just to come round and knock on my door.

He was right, they were big scary men and they obviously didn't like him. They looked at me sideways, as if trying to work out my relationship with the puny little fellow who stood at the stern of their vessel with a small cardboard box clutched to his chest. A silver-haired official from the MUA gave a short speech eulogising the life and achievements of their departed comrade as we cruised down the placid Port River. As we passed by the ship being loaded at the cement works we gave two ear-splitting blasts of our siren to be echoed by that vessel, in turn followed by that of a bulk grain carrier moored on the opposite side of the river. A sailor's farewell.

Shane stepped forward, opened his box and emptied the dusty contents into the churned up water which swirled and eddied at our stern. Seagulls cried and screamed in frustration on finding nothing edible trailing in our wake. Somewhere off to starboard a dolphin's fin broke the surface before it raised its beak and arched its back in preparation for a deep dive. We returned to port and I accompanied Shane home. That was the last time that I saw the strange little fellow.

I heard him, however, over the next few days, crying sometimes on the other side of the fence, whilst I laboured preparing our new garden. I pictured him in his hermetic enclosure, pacing out his sorrow on the pristine lawn, like some cloistered medieval monk communing with God, or maybe with the spirits of the dead. After a few days I heard him no more. When a week had gone by with no further sign I went round and knocked on his door. Receiving no reply, worried, eventually I rang the police. They found him, apparently still sitting in an armchair, an empty can of beer in his hand.

"They call them soupers," Michael at work said once he had read about it in the paper, and he laughed.

"What?" I asked him.

"Emergency services. When they find a body that's been dead a little while. They call them soupers, because of the bodily fluids," and he gave another laugh. I know I shouldn't have done it but I couldn't help myself. I reached back and then smacked him one right in the mouth.

ABOUT EDDY KNIGHT

Eddy Knight was born and raised in Britain's West Country, arriving in South Australia in 1990. He worked for many years as a bench hand joiner, before becoming an actor and then a theatre director. He has worked with Howard Barker's The Wrestling School, both in the U.K. and for the 2000 Adelaide Festival, the Bell Shakespeare Company, Red Stitch Actors' Theatre, State Theatre of South Australia, Brink, and many of Adelaide's semi-professional companies. Having had two plays produced locally and in New Zealand and come runner up in a couple of literary competitions, he was offered a place in the Creative Writing program of the University of Adelaide, gaining a PhD in 2017. In 2018 he was shortlisted in the Alan Marshall short story competition, had stories published on the Tablo.io/eddy-knight website and in 2019 had stories published in Pure Slush's *Envy* and *Pride* 7 Deadly Sins anthologies and one in Truth Serum Press's *Stories My Gay Uncle Told Me*. He is a member of the Adelaide Writers' Group and lives with his partner and two Siamese cats close to the sea in Port Adelaide.

ACKNOWLEDGEMENTS

The majority of the stories in this cycle were written while I was studying for a PhD in creative writing at the University of Adelaide. When I first fronted up as a very mature student, unsure, ignorant of what would be required of me and overawed by what might lie ahead, my supervisor Dr. Phillip Edmonds told me to 'just walk on the beach for a while.' He assured me that 'it'll soon come to you.' Semaphore to Largs and on up to North Haven has one of the loveliest stretches of beach with the softest golden sand that I have ever walked upon, and luckily is very close to where I live. He was so right, and I thank him for his suggestion and his support. These stories are the result of those walks.

I must thank Dr. Philip Butterss for his geniality, support and proof-reading skills and also Professor Brian Castro for his friendship, encouragement and positive response to my stories. Particularly I have to thank the University of Adelaide and the Australian Government for the scholarship which allowed me to devote my time to this project.

Above all else I have to thank my partner Justene, not only for her constant belief in my talent, but also for encouraging me to apply for the scholarship in the first place, when I was at a particularly low ebb.

Having been the first person in my family ever to go to university, to end up with a doctorate quite astounds me. I could only wish that my parents were still alive to see the day that their sacrifices on my behalf finally bore fruit.

A further acknowledgement is due to the playwright, poet and director of the Wrestling School theatre company, Howard Barker, who has been something of an inspiration to me ever since I came across his *Arguments for a Theatre* in a New Zealand bookshop in 1990. That day and that work could be said to have changed my life, leading me eventually to becoming a director myself.

To every actor I have ever had the pleasure to act alongside or to direct, I thank you all for your friendship and encouragement and for the lessons that I have learnt from every one of you.

The Author was first published by Pure Slush Books, in the anthology *Envy 7 Deadly Sins Vol 6*, 2019.

The Consultation was first published by Tablo.io on the website Eddy-Knight, 2017.

Also from TRUTH SERUM PRESS

https://truthserumpress.net/catalogue/

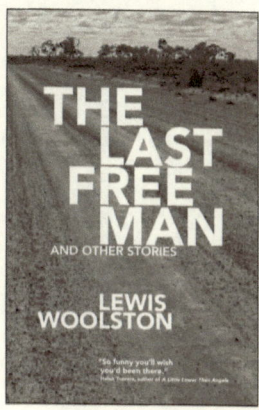  

- *The Last Free Man* by Lewis Woolston
  978-1-925536-88-1 (paperback) 978-1-925536-89-8 (eBook)
- *Stories My Gay Uncle Told Me* *Truth Serum Vol. 3*
  978-1-925536-86-7 (paperback) 978-1-925536-87-4 (eBook)
- *Easy Money* by Steve Evans
  978-1-925536-81-2 (paperback) 978-1-925536-82-9 (eBook)

- *Minotaur and Other Stories* by Salvatore Difalco
  978-1-925536-79-9 (paperback) 978-1-925536-80-5 (eBook)
- *The Story of the Milkman* by Alan Walowitz
  978-1-925536-76-8 (paperback) 978-1-925536-77-5 (eBook)
- *The Book of Acrostics* by John Lambremont, Sr.
  978-1-925536-52-2 (paperback) 978-1-925536-53-9 (eBook)

Also from TRUTH SERUM PRESS

https://truthserumpress.net/catalogue/

- *Square Pegs* by Rob Walker
  978-1-925536-62-1 (paperback) 978-1-925536-63-8 (eBook)
- *Cheat Sheets* by Edward O'Dwyer
  978-1-925536-60-7 (paperback) 978-1-925536-61-4 (eBook)
- *The Crazed Wind* by Nod Ghosh
  978-1-925536-58-4 (paperback) 978-1-925536-59-1 (eBook)

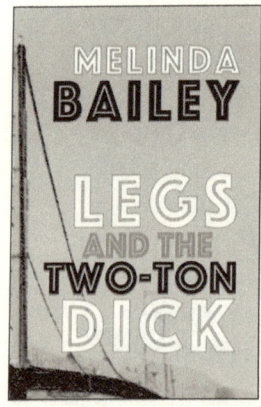  

- *Legs and the Two-Ton Dick* by Melinda Bailey
  978-1-925536-37-9 (paperback) 978-1-925536-38-6 (eBook)
- *Dollhouse Masquerade* by Samuel E. Cole
  978-1-925536-43-0 (paperback) 978-1-925536-44-7 (eBook)
- *Kiss Kiss* by Paul Beckman
  978-1-925536-21-8 (paperback) 978-1-925536-22-5 (eBook)

Also from TRUTH SERUM PRESS

https://truthserumpress.net/catalogue/

  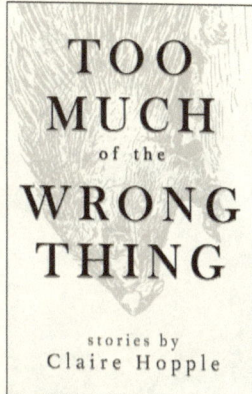

- *Inklings* by Irene Buckler
  978-1-925536-41-6 (paperback) 978-1-925536-42-3 (eBook)
- *On the Bitch* by Matt Potter
  978-1-925536-45-4 (paperback) 978-1-925536-46-1 (eBook)
- *Too Much of the Wrong Thing* by Claire Hopple
  978-1-925536-33-1 (paperback) 978-1-925536-34-8 (eBook)

- *Track Tales* by Mercedes Webb-Pullman
  978-1-925536-35-5 (paperback) 978-1-925536-36-2 (eBook)
- *Luck and Other Truths* by Richard Mark Glover
  978-1-925101-77-5 (paperback) 978-1-925536-04-1 (eBook)
- *Hello Berlin!* by Jason S. Andrews
  978-1-925536-11-9 (paperback) 978-1-925536-12-6 (eBook)

Also from TRUTH SERUM PRESS

https://truthserumpress.net/catalogue/

 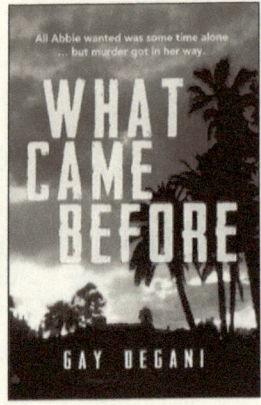 

- *Deer Michigan* by Jack C. Buck
  978-1-925536-25-6 (paperback) 978-1-925536-26-3 (eBook)
- *What Came Before* by Gay Degani
  978-1-925536-05-8 (paperback) 978-1-925536-06-5 (eBook)
- *Rain Check* by Levi Andrew Noe
  978-1-925536-09-6 (paperback) 978-1-925536-10-2 (eBook)

 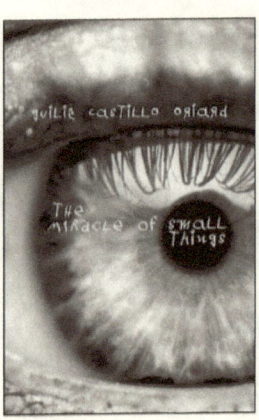 

- *Based on True Stories* by Matt Potter
  978-1-925101-75-1 (paperback) 978-1-925101-76-8 (eBook)
- *The Miracle of Small Things* by Guilie Castillo Oriard
  978-1-925101-73-7 (paperback) 978-1-925101-74-4 (eBook)
- *La Ronde* by Townsend Walker
  978-1-925101-64-5 (paperback) 978-1-925101-65-2 (eBook)